TEXAS FISTS

JACKSON COLE

WHEELER PUBLISHING
A part of Gale, Cengage Learning

D1502740

GALE
CENGAGE Learning

Detroit • New York • San Francisco • New Haven, Conn • Waterville, Maine • London

GALE
CENGAGE Learning®

LIBRARY OF CONGRESS CATALOGING-IN-PUBLICATION DATA

Cole, Jackson.
    Texas fists / by Jackson Cole. — Large print ed.
        p. cm. — (Wheeler Publishing large print western)
    "A Jim Hatfield Western."
    ISBN 978-1-4104-5289-4 (pbk.) — ISBN 1-4104-5289-1 (pbk.) 1. Hatfield, Jim
(Fictitious character)—Fiction. 2. Texas Rangers—Fiction. 3. Outlaws—Fiction.
4. Texas—Fiction. 5. Large type books. I. Title.
PS3505.O2685T48 2012
813'.54—dc23   2012030057

Published in 2012 by arrangement with Golden Western Literary
Agency.

Printed in the United States of America
    1 2 3 4 5   16 15 14 13 12

ED297

TEXAS FISTS

CHAPTER I

It was shadowy between the tall trunks that shot up to where the mighty branches of the pines formed the roof of nature's own majestic cathedral. A carpet of warm brown covered the earth. Here and there patches of undergrowth strove to reach the sun that was shut away by the waving crown of needles far above. Infrequent gulleys told of rain water rushing down the slope when the green "roofs" tossed against a stormy sky and the wind shook a terrible music from the giant harp of the trees.

Shadows and silence — the restful silence whose broad base of muted sound was the sighing of a million needles and the gentle rubbing of branch on branch. The shadows were cool and blue, their edges ragged as they rippled in the faint breeze.

Suddenly a shaft of glowing sunlight shot between the trunks, cleaving the shadows as with a sword of gold, turning the brown needle carpet to rich amber splashed with molten bronze. The trunks became towering spires of burnished copper. The green ceiling changed to trembling amethyst.

On either side of the golden sword the shadows were purple edged with ruby. They melted back to rich cobalt, faded to an azure mist, and were lost amid the crowding trunks that were like silent spectators awaiting a pageant of Valkyrie to march along that Bifrost Bridge, sharp as a sword-edge, of fiery gold.

But instead of star-eyed battle maidens shepherding the souls of the slain to Valhalla, there rode along the golden path a man on a horse whose coat, in the sunset light, seemed to be of shimmering flame. Full eighteen hands high he stood, mighty of barrel, long of limb, fining to exquisite lines of dainty breed in neck and head. His liquid eyes were filled with fire and intelligence, his hoofs were small, clean-cut as the back of a razor. Mane and tail were deepest glossy black.

The tall rider of the tall horse was as noteworthy as his mount. Full four inches more than six feet, and though seeming spare to the eye, his girth matched his height. Broad shoulders and deep chest tapered to the slim waist and flat hips of perfect physical condition. His hawk-face was deeply bronzed, his eyes gray-green like the needles of the pines. His rather wide mouth quirked cheerfully at the corners and there was a ripple of muscle along the angle of his lean jaw. Those quirked corners somewhat relieved the grimness of the powerful chin beneath the wide mouth and the tinge of fierceness evinced in the high-bridged nose and the prominent cheek-bones.

The man's garb was the homely costume of the rangeland, but he wore it as Coeur de Lion must have worn armor. Dark shirt, its somberness relieved by the brilliant handkerchief looped about the sinewy throat, sagging vest, overalls, shotgun chaps of tanned leather. His high-heeled boots were likewise of soft leather. Encircling the lean waist were filled double-cartridge belts, and from the carefully worked and oiled cut-out holsters protruded the black butts of heavy guns.

They were worn unusually low, those long-barreled guns, their muzzles tapping against the rider's muscular thighs, the holsters slung loosely so that the slightest wrist motion would flare the plain wooden grips away from the wearer's sides and ready to the slim, steely-fingered hands.

A wide-brimmed "J.B." high as to dimpled crown, completed the outfit. The hair above the broad forehead, revealed by the pushed-back hat, was thick and black.

Quite a few years before, the tall man with the strangely colored eyes had sat in the office of Captain Bill McDowell, the "Grand Old Man" of the Rangers, and listened to the quiet voice of the commander of the Frontier Legion, as the great Border Post of the Rangers was known.

"I know how you feel, Jim," said Captain Bill. "I know your dad was killed by wide-loopers who ran off his herd. A snake-blooded killing if there ever was one. I know you're out to ride the vengeance trail, to get those hellions. But, Jim, taking the law into your own hands is a mighty risky business. One little slip and all of a sudden you find *you're* riding the outlaw trail. Let's see, now, you took civil engineering in college, I believe."

"That's right, suh," replied the ice-eyed, bleak-faced young man across from him.

"And did considerable work at it during vacation days."

"Right again, suh, and some railroading and mine work, acquiring knowledge necessary to an engineer when he gets into field work on his own. Mavericked around quite a bit, too, down in Mexico, over in New Mexico and Arizona, and other places.

Captain Bill nodded. "Speak Spanish pretty well, I understand?" Jim Hatfield nodded.

"And know cattle work up and down."

"I was born and brought up on a spread, as you know," Hatfield agreed.

"Yes, I know all that," admitted the Ranger Captain. "Knew your dad for years, and, knowing him as I did, I know the blood you got in you — a hot, wild blood, like you find in most jiggers of Virginia and Kentuck stock. Know, too, you seem to have inherited your dad's size, and his gunslinging ability. Anse Hatfield was said by lots of folks to have the fastest gunhand in Texas. Hear you're even a mite faster, and a natural two-gun man. Understand you draw and shoot equally well with either hand. Most two-gun packers use the left one as a sort of reserve, and do all their plugging with the right hand iron until that one's empty."

Hatfield shot the Captain a puzzled glance. "What the devil was the old fire-eater leading up to?" he wondered.

"All of which brings me down to the point," concluded Captain Bill. "You've got the qualifications needed to make a smart and successful engineer, which I figure you will, eventually. You also got the qualifications for something else."

"What's that?" Hatfield asked curiously.

"A Texas Ranger," Captain Bill said quietly.

Hatfield stared at him. "Meaning?"

"Meaning that I'm offering you a chance to run down your dad's killers — in the right way. With all the power and prestige of the State of Texas behind you. As a Ranger you can do it without taking the chance of finding yourself one with the men you're after. Which is what I'm thinking of. So, come into the Rangers. It's something of an honor, to be offered a job with the Rangers. We're just a mite particular who we take in with us, as you may have heard. Running down your dad's killers will be your first chore. Of course, after you finish with that you can resign and go back to engineering," he added craftily.

Hatfield considered for some moments. Then the first smile that had lighted his face for a week suddenly flashed his white even teeth.

"Reckon, suh," he said, "you've hired yourself a hand."

But by the time the men who had killed his father were brought to justice — and it was a long and arduous chase — Jim Hatfield found that something had happened to him. He had found his life work. He was — *a Ranger!*

And now the Lone Wolf, as a stern old Lieutenant of Rangers had dubbed him, was legend throughout Texas and the whole Southwest. The Ranger who never failed. The Ranger who could not be killed. Honored and respected by honest men. Feared and hated by the owlhoot breed. Bill McDowell's Lieutenant and ace-man: The *Lone Wolf!*

Lounging carelessly in his saddle, as one who has spent his life on horseback, Jim Hatfield rode along the sun-drenched path, narrowing his black-lashed lids to the glare, seeming oblivious to all about him, but in reality missing nothing.

The path between the tree trunks narrowed, the tall spires crowding closer and closer to one another, as if jealous of the drafty spaces through which the wind sighed and the sunlight gleamed. Underbrush began to replace the monotonous brown carpet. The path became a walled corridor of russet and gray and mottled green. From time to time the horseman was forced to bow his tall head to escape brushing branch or frond. And as the path narrowed, the gloom became more intense, pressing in upon the dimming bar of sunlight, its edges clean-cut jade.

Hatfield rode, talked lazily to the horse at intervals, swaying lithely to the animal's every move, seemingly listless, drowsing in the arms of the sunset.

Like a released steel spring, he snapped into action. His hand tensed on the reins, legs like bands of brass clamped the horse's middle, the lazy voice blared forth a trumpet call:

"On, Goldy!"

Instantly the great sorrel shot forward — straight into the path of rushing, crackling death — under the downward plunging trunk of one of the forest giants which stood a scant score of feet from the brush walled trail.

It seemed the toppling column grazed horse and rider. Then the tremendous sweep of massive branches roared downward to triumph where the thundering trunk had failed. The displaced air screeched like a thousand furies under the stab of a million tossing needles.

With a crashing roar the great tree reached the earth. A kaleidoscope of sun motes gleamed and flickered as the needles flew in a sparkling dust. Twigs and splinters hurtled far and wide. Shattered branches whizzed outward like projectiles from great guns, shredding the brush wall, thudding against standing trunks whose brown pillars showed instant fleckings of sappy white.

The golden horse squealed as a reaching frond whipped his glossy haunch. The rider reeled beneath the rushing sweep of a massive branch. For a crawling instant of terror, horse and man seemed engulfed in the foam of green and gray. Then the big cayuse streaked from beneath the hurtling death and before the last echoes had ceased to slam back and forth between the trunks, his rider had pulled him to a snorting, whistling halt, a score of yards from the smashed path of destruction.

Hatfield breathed deeply, and exhaled from his great chest. He rubbed a bronzed cheek that still stung from the lash of angry twigs, straightened his hat on his black head and turned to gaze back at the death which had missed its stroke by inches.

"Feller," he said quietly, "that sign we passed a mile or so back meant what it said!"

For another moment or so the golden horse's reddened eye continued to roll, his nostrils to flare. Then he quieted, his flattened ears pricked forward once more and he tossed an inquiring head.

"Just a minute," Hatfield told him. "I've a notion it wouldn't be time wasted to look things over." He walked the cayuse back to the welter of smashed branches, pulled him to a halt once more and stared at the scene of destruction.

Something in the appearance of the sea of needles narrowed his strangely-colored eyes and deepened the concentration furrow between his black brows. With the lithe motion of a relaxing panther, he dismounted. Intensely interested, he bent over a projecting jumble of twigs. There was a hard ripple of knotty muscle along his lean jaw as he straightened up and and his wide mouth, ordinarily good-humoredly quirked at the corners, was a hard, straight line.

The eyes, too, had subtly changed color. They were no longer the warm green of sunlight glinting on the cheerful waters of a summer sea. They were now the color of that same sea when it heaves ominously under a slaty sky and the bleak winds of winter wail beneath their prison roof of snow-flecked cloud. He spoke to his horse, as man speaks to man, and his voice was like the rasp of a steel tire on ice —

"Uh-huh, I was right. Those needles are brown at the tips of the branches."

His glance traveled toward where the great

crown of the tree lay tangled in a welter of smashed undergrowth. He nodded to the horse, the look of stern satisfaction on his face intensifying.

"Whole top browned and wilted," he said. "Tree's been dead for days, and the green of the needles farther along the branches shows it didn't die gradually. Let's look a little more, feller."

He worked his way through the tangle of growth to where the splintered stump stood with one jagged spire extending some ten feet into the air. Here he paused, a puzzled expression on his bronzed face.

The side of the stump farthest from the trail was hollowed out, apparently by fire. The concave depression was deeply charred, the burning extending from within a few inches of the ground to a height of some five or six feet. Midway the burned section had been eaten almost through by the flames and it appeared remarkable that the trunk remained standing as long as it did.

"Appears like a little breeze would have been enough to topple her," he mused. "Looks like she was well hollowed out by rot, then fire came along and finished the job. Reckon the jar of Goldy's hoofs was enough to send her over."

He eyed the burned section, his gaze

travelling upward along the jagged splinter. And as he gazed, the green eyes narrowed once again.

"Sure burned even," he muttered.

Stepping closer to the stump, he stooped and stared intently at the charred concave. Slipping a knife from his pocket, he carefully scraped the char — scraped until a spot of clean white wood was revealed. He leaned even closer, searching the white surface in the fading light.

Suddenly his peering eyes blazed. He rubbed the white surface with a sensitive finger, probed a tiny slit with a nail. Abruptly he desisted and resumed scraping with the knife — in the very center of the regular concave. A moment later, a wordless sound of satisfaction escaped his lips.

The char, which was remarkably shallow for a burned-out trunk, had been scraped away to reveal a deep cut in the white surface of the underlying wood — a cut that drove inward to almost reach the bark on the far side of the trunk.

"Chopped!" he muttered, snapping shut the blade of his knife. "Chopped with an axe. Chopped almost through, then carefully burned to look like rot and fire was responsible. Only," he added grimly, staring at the tell-tale gash, "they didn't burn quite deep enough. Reckon, though, they figured the gent underneath that mess wouldn't be in any shape to do any prying around."

Which was indubitably true. Only his own uncanny keenness of perception, aided and abetted by perfect coordination of brain and muscle, had saved him from the fate intended by that downward plunging trunk. That and the catlike agility of the great golden horse.

Hatfield turned to where the vanishing sunlight turned the tall sorrel's coat to molten bronze.

"Thanks, feller," he said simply.

He turned back again to the stump. He sidled around it, until he was beneath the jagged butt of the fallen tree. In the deepening shadow he groped amid the crushed branches. With a grunt of satisfaction he drew forth a length of stout timber, its ends notched in a peculiar way. Directly in line with the trunk he found a second timber, driven slantwise deeply into the ground. The upper end of this timber was splintered as from a terrific blow, and near its middle a deep notch was cut.

Hatfield lifted the first timber and placed it in the notch. It fitted snugly.

"That's what held the trunk up," he muttered. "Regular 'figure-four' trap like kids use to trap rabbits with. Now where's the third side of the four? Bet it's got a rope tied to it!"

Another moment of searching discovered the missing section of the trap. It, too, was notched at one end, but fastened to the end which would normally be pointed for the bait — the end which extended beyond the hypotenuse side of the trap, was a stout wire cable.

Hatfield followed the line of the cable, to where it vanished in a small hole beside the trail. He seized it and tugged strongly. The cable tautened, resisted his efforts. He put forth his strength and the wire responded reluctantly.

"Heavy weight fastened to the end of it," he muttered, letting the wire spring back.

He forced his way through the obstructing growth and reached the trail. Pausing, he stamped on the innocent appearing carpet of needles. A hollow boom rewarded the act and he could feel the apparently solid ground sag springily under his feet.

"That's it," he muttered, his bronzed face bleak. "Step here, right close to where the tree stood, your weight sinks the grounds a little — reckon the dirt rests on springy boards — a rock or something rolls off balance in the hole down there and jerks the cable fastened to the trap. The trap slips from under the almost cut-through trunk, and down comes the tree. Simple in principle, but a mighty ingenious way to commit a murder. And if it wasn't for these sticks and the wire, there wouldn't be any evidence there *was* a murder. Would look like an accident. Wonder who they were after. Not me, that's sure for certain. I just hit the section, and this thing was rigged up several days ago. What the —"

His keen ears caught the sound of a stick snapping under a stealthy foot. With catlike agility, he flung himself backward toward the growth and even as he did so, a gun cracked, its echoes slamming back and forth between the trunks.

Hatfield's tall figure crashed into the growth, slumped limply to the ground and was still, a dim, uncertain shape amid the shadows under the tangle of fronds and branches.

And from between the tree trunks beyond the trail, purposeful shadows stole cautiously toward the motionless form. The last dying light of the sunset glinted evilly on the barrels of ready guns.

Chapter II

There was an air of expectation in Espantosa. It hung, miasma-like, over the town as the ghostly mists hang over the sullen pools in Espantosa Canyon to the west and south of the town. Espantosa — "haunted canyon" — the Spanish Conquistadores named the gloomy, sinister gorge, with good reason, and the C & P railroad builders named the town after the canyon.

A strange town, Espantosa. The saloon bars glittered with glass and mirrors. The dancehall floors were wide and smooth. The appointments of the gambling hells were varied and intricate. The shops were abundantly stocked. The dusty streets, with their rough board sidewalks, were thronged with colorful figures. But nowhere was to be seen a substantial or imposing building. It was a town of hastily thrown together wooden structures, clapboard tar-paper shacks, rude log cabins with chinks between the logs unfilled even with mud, dirty canvas tents. It looked as if it had just "happaned" over night and was likely to vanish with the light of any dawn.

Which was exactly the case. Espantosa was a railroad construction town, ready to move on when railhead had progressed so far westward as to make its site inconvenient for the horde of workers who dwelt there and to whom it owed its precarious existence. Each morning the long construction trains thundered westward with their loads of track layers, sleepy-eyed, sullen, grumpy. Each evening they steamed back into the yards with the same workers cheerful and chattery, eyes agleam with anticipation, itching for the boisterous pleasures the town afforded.

Hardly a day passed, however, when one or more of those who rode out in the morning did not ride back at night. Railroad building in this wild land was a hazardous business under normal conditions, and conditions in the Espantosa country were far from normal.

North and east of the town was a vast belt of forest. Here the tall pines stood as plumed chiefs, with groves of gnarled oaks like toil-bowed attendants to the upright majesty of the conifers.

For age on age, the music of the wind in the silence of the woodland had been broken only by the wail of the coyote, the howl of the timber wolf, the mournful plaint of the owl and the scream of the cougar. But now new and strange sounds had come to shatter the eternal peace. The rasp of saw tooth, the ringing clash of ax blade, the chatter of the donkey engine, and the shouts of men.

For the C & P, skirting the fringe of the woodland, and the L & W, farther to the south, needed timber for crossties, for cribbing, for buildings. The green of the needles and the leaves had turned to gold — gold in a rich flood that poured into the pockets of men with foresight, energy and daring. And borne on the turbulent breast of this flood came hatred and greed and all the sinister passions attendant to those primal emotions that seethe in the breasts of men.

To the south was rangeland, green and bronze and amethyst and amber. Here grew needle and wheat grasses, rich in the stored-up energy of the great Texas sun and the sweet rains of the dry country. Here grazed great herds of long-horned, plump-sided steers, wild of eye, savage as to disposition. The coming of the rival railroads had turned these slow-moving herds also to a broad river of gold.

Gold! Lumbermen and ranchers were reaping a rich harvest. As were others lured here into the wild lands by the glitter of the siren metal which is yellow with the dust of dry bones and red with splashings of blood.

There were plenty of these "others" in the hell town of Espantosa. There had always been plenty of them in this hole-in-the-wall country between the Rio Grande and the High Plains, where the Nuecos flows, where the Apaches and the Lipans made their most desperate stand against the encroaching Comanches and a few Spanish rancheros built fortified homes and stocked the country with horses and cattle which were soon to run wild and unclaimed. So numerous became the bands of maverick horses that on the early maps, the word "mustang" described the wide blank.

Here bandits of two languages raided and met and defied capture. Just as "no law west of the Pecos" came to describe the outlaw country farther west, so "the deadline for sheriffs" was a synonym for this vast stretch of Texas across which all traffic from Mexico to the interior of the state ran, and where the trains of carts and pack animals to New Orleans and St. Louis ambled with outriders grim and watchful, with scouts and rear guard gripping ready rifle and six-gun.

Between the rangeland and the river, vast thickets of thorned brush, prickly pear and dagger provided ambush and concealment. On the desert grew the cactus in a hundred varieties, the greasewood and the sage.

Espantosa, just south of the timber country, named for the ghost canyon of death and blood, became the gathering place of those who rode the wastelands' dim trails. And in the wake of the fingers of steel, questing out of the east, came as motley and sinister a crew as that which drifted northward from the gleaming river or out of the weird jumble of spire and chimney rock and harshly-colored buttes that sentinelled the badlands to the west.

There were two reasons for the air of expectancy that hovered over Espantosa. The first was a monthly occurrence. Bartenders polished glasses, saw that full bottles were ready to hand out and made their reserve stocks ample. In the dance-halls, the girls laid out their gayest and shortest dresses, deepened the red of already too-red cheeks and lips. The gamblers overhauled their paraphernalia and made sure that "percentages" were what they should be. The sheriff, up from the county seat and installed in his temporary office, oiled his guns and swore in additional deputies.

All this was largely routine, for tomorrow was pay day for the railroad workers and hell aplenty would bust loose before another sun had set. By singular "co-incidence," pay day for the lumber camps and for the ranches to the south always managed to fall on railroad pay days of late; which provided more festivity in Espantosa, and more trouble for the sheriff.

In addition to pay day, however, was expected a much-discussed "announcement" by General Manager James G. ("Jaggers") Dunn of the C & P, the "Empire Builder." Just what would be the precise nature of the announcement was not known, but it *was* known by all that upon that announcement hinged the fate and future of the town.

"Him and Austin Flint of Texco Lumber had a long talk over to the C & P office yesterday mornin'," Runt McCarthy, head bartender at the Sluicegates Saloon, informed eager listeners. "Then Vane of Cibola Timber Co. dropped in and him and Flint got to slangin' each other per usual. Dunn was sort of put out, I understand. Said it was bad enough for two railroads to be feudin' like the C & P and the L & W are without local outfits being on the prod against each other."

An attentive cattleman exploded an exasperated oath.

"Brush Vane is a detriment to this section," he declared. "Austin Flint's a gent if there ever was one, but Vane's a reg'lar old shorthorn. He's had his own way so many years and been so used to making other folks do as he says, he thinks he's the big skookum he-wolf of the pack and always will be. Well, he's got another think coming or I'm a heap mistaken. Folks have stood about all from that old snorter they're goin' to, you mark my words."

"Vane's salty," remarked another. "He's a cold proposition, Cal. I wouldn't go shootin' off my head so promiscuous if I was you."

The cattleman flushed darkly red. He downed his drink at a gulp, sucked the drops from his drooping moustache with a savage hiss and growled deep in his hairy chest.

"To hell with Brush Vane and everything he represents!" he exclaimed harshly. "I tell you this country's getting almighty tired of being run by his kind, and the time's coming, and soon, when we're going to put a stop to it — and to Brush Vane, too. You mark my words!"

Silence and a nervous shifting of feet followed this declaration in a voice that rang through the big room. Some glanced uneasily at the swinging doors and the open windows. Others began to take great interest in their drinks. The bartender moved down the bar and industriously polished glasses. He started jerkily, flinging his head up as a clatter of hoofs, followed by shouts,

28

sounded in the street outside the saloon.

"It's the Slash K boys riding in," said a young puncher, peering out of the window.

"And that'll mean more hell!" grumbled the bartender.

"I got a hunch Brush Vane'd done better to stick to his Slash K ranch and not get mixed up in the lumber business," observed a young cowboy.

"Can't you hellions find somethin' else to talk about besides Brush Vane?" the bartender demanded querulously.

"I was just aiming to point out a cowman usually tangles his rope when he branches out into other things," the cowboy replied.

"Uh-huh, other things — like wideloop-ing, smuggling, promiscuous killings and such," sarcastically put in the cattleman named Cal.

Again there was silence about the bar. Farther down the street sounded more yells, and a stutter of shots.

"Sheriff Rider'll be on the prod for sure," chuckled the cowboy. "I got a notion the Slash K boys got their pay this evening before they rode in. Anyway, they're sure beginning to whoop her up. Listen to 'em howl!"

The big cattleman downed another drink, hiccoughed loudly and lurched from the bar. He wandered about the room unsteadily for a few minutes. The others at the bar cast furtive glances in his direction from time to time. Finally, after staring truculently at a roulette wheel for a spell, he slouched to a window which opened onto an alley skirting the side of the saloon building. He stood with his broad back to the bar, glowering into the darkness.

"Cal has sure been on the prod against Brush Vane, ever since Brush horned in and took that beef contract with the L & W away from him," observed one of the drinkers at the bar in low tones.

"I reckon Vane was inside his rights, takin' that order from Cal," a companion replied in the same voice, "but just the same it does sort of get under a feller's skin when a jigger shoves a littler feller aside and hogs everything just because he's big enough to do it. Appears to me Vane could have let Cal go on selling what steers he had to the L & W, instead of insisting the railroad'd have to contract to buy everything from him if they wanted him to sell to them at all. Reckon you can't blame the railroad, though. They got to have meat, and Cal and the other little spread they were dealin' with couldn't s'ply 'em with 'nough critters in a hurry when they needed 'em, and Vane could."

"Uh-huh, but Vane tried to run the same kind of whizzer with the C & P, and old Jaggers Dunn told him to go to hell."

"Dunn's a salty old maverick himself, and ain't used to taking orders from nobody. There's sure trouble building up between him and Cosgrove of the L & W. Fact is, it looks like this section is in for more merry hell than ordinary, and that's saying plenty. I hear tell some folks are already yelling to Bill McDowell to send over a company of Rangers."

"Swell chance! What with the way things are on the border and the Panhandle boilin' over, and them Oklahoma outfits busting banks and robbing stages. The Rangers have got other things to do besides mix up in a local row like this between railroad builders and lumber camps and cow outfits. Reckon it's up to Sheriff Rider."

The other snorted contemptuously. "Honest," he apostrophized the sheriff. "Honest, and dumb, and stubborn as a blue-nosed mule. Nobody could convince Nat Rider that there's anything about Brush Vane that ain't hunky-dory. He —"

A roaring explosion shook the room. From the dark alley beyond the open window gushed twin lances of reddish flame. Cal Hudgins, the cattleman who had been so outspoken against Brush Vane, seemed to be literally blown away from the window by those double spears of lurid light. He catapulted backwards, thudded to the floor, writhed for a bloody moment and was still.

For a crawling instant, men froze in grotesque positions, paralyzed by the grim tragedy they had witnessed. Then, as swift feet sounded in the alley, they leaped for the window, bawling curses. Guns roared and banged into the dark. Some of the boldest leaped across the sill and pounded after those vanished footsteps that had echoed the shotgun blast.

Others gathered about the body of the dead Cal Hudgins.

"Blowed plumb in two!" said one in an awed voice. "A sawed-off gun, both barrels loaded with slugs. Reckon Cal never knew what hit him!"

"No more than Ace Simon knew last month when he was dry-gulched in Espantosa Canyon," said a bitter voice. "Ace had trouble with Brush Vane, too, if you fellers recollect. Poor ol' Cal, I told him he hadn't ought to sound off so promiscuous about Brush Vane. He —"

The speaker's voice trickled to mouthy

silence and his tongue clove to the roof of his mouth as a deep rumble sounded from the outer doorway:

"What about Brush Vane?"

CHAPTER III

Denser and denser grew the shadows among the towering trunks of the pines. And ever more cautiously those moving shadows with the last faint gleams of light glinting from their ready gun barrels stole toward the motionless huddle under the fallen pine. So vague and uncertain was the body of the man who had fallen before the blast of gunfire that none of the stealthy stalkers could say for sure just where it lay. But emboldened by the silence and the stillness, they stepped forth more briskly, caution abating. For an instant their crouching forms stood out hard and clear against the tremulous glow still seeping down the brush-walled trail.

From the bristle of branches and needles gushed streams of yellowish flame. A staccato drum roll of reports ricocheted from trunk to trunk.

One of the crouching stalkers flung erect, screaming shrilly. He went down, thrashing and writhing in the brush. A second pitched forward with a queer little grunt and lay sprawled in the trail. A third yelled a pain-maddened curse, jutted his gun forward and curled his finger on the trigger. Then he yelled again, in pain and fury, as the gun, its lock smashed, its grip spattered with blood, spun from his hand and vanished amid the growth. Behind him sounded a prodigious smashing and crackling as his two companions who still remained on their feet tore through the growth in panic-stricken flight.

Still bawling curses, he whirled and pounded after them, whining slugs speeding him on his way.

Face grim, guns ready, Hatfield rose from behind the log which had sheltered him. With the back of his hand he felt of the oozing welt just below his left temple. Barely in time had he flung himself sideways and down the instant before the dry-gulcher's gun had cracked.

"Inch more to the right and it'd been trail's end," he muttered, his gaze intent on the silent forms beside the trail, his ears straining to catch any intimation that the remaining killers had paused in their flight.

But the crashings died away gradually in a faint, far snapping of twigs as the dry-gulchers put distance between themselves and the deadly guns. *They* didn't know it was Captain McDowell's ace man they had tried to down, but they knew they had grabbed a mountain lion by the tail, and they were damned anxious to let go!

For another moment, Hatfield listened, then he cautiously approached the forms sprawled in the trail.

There was no need for caution. The men were thoroughly and satisfactorily dead. Hatfield squatted beside the first and peered into a dark, distorted face with lank black hair hanging over the forehead almost to the glazing beady eyes.

"Yaqui halfbreed, judging from the look of him," he muttered, his gaze shifting to the second dry-gulcher, whose bulky form was agonizingly twisted, his broad countenance stamped by a ferocity not even death could obliterate.

"And this one is full-blood Apache, or I'm a heap mistaken," the Ranger added. "And both dressed civilized."

With deft fingers he went through the pockets of the dead men, turning out a miscellany of rubbish of little significance. There was some money in gold and silver coin, knives and other trinkets. A flat metal disc carried by the lean half-breed attracted his attention. On its surface was stamped a number and in the last fading gleams of the sunset, Hatfield could make out a curving line of raised letters, which spelled: *Cibola Timber Co.*

Here was something that caused the Ranger's strangely-colored eyes to narrow slightly and his lean jaw to tighten.

"Worker's identification tag with his payroll number," he catalogued the bit of metal. "Sorta looks like this punctured gent was employed by the Cibola Timber Co. Hmmm!"

He recalled again the sign posted at the point where the trail entered the woodland —

CIBOLA TIMBER CO.
Keep Out
DANGER

"Uh-huh," he repeated what he had told the horse the moment after their narrow escape from the falling tree, "uh-huh, that sign sure meant what it said. But just the same it doesn't make sense. Appears to me anybody might be liable to cut along that trail, so why go to all that trouble to drop a tree trunk on him? And then have jiggers creeping up to make sure of the job?"

He gingerly felt of the slight wound on his head, turned the tag in slim, bronzed fingers, and nodded to himself.

"What those jiggers were creeping up for was not particularly to make sure they'd gotten the feller they were after, but to remove the evidence," he told himself grimly. "With that figure four trap out of sight, there wouldn't be a thing to show the gent squashed under the tree wasn't cashed in by natural causes. Sure looks like the Cibola Timber Company doesn't want visitors to happen along unexpected — or maybe some *particular* visitor. Reckon old Captain Bill was right, per usual, when he said there were some almighty funny things happening over in this section, and that a Ranger wouldn't be a bit welcome."

With a last glance at the silent forms, he walked lithely to his waiting horse, mounted and settled himself in the saddle. He gazed down the dark tunnel of the trail for a moment, and shook his head.

"A short-cut is sometimes the longest way around," he told Goldy as he turned the sorrel's head toward the straggly wall of brush.

Goldy didn't like it, but he forced his way through, snorting his indignation from time to time. Once away from the trail, the going was easier and an hour later they came out onto a wagon road boring south by west.

Far up the slope was a flicker of lights and to Hatfield's keen ears came the thin whine of a distant sawmill.

He did not turn toward the lumber camp, however, and the sorrel jogged comfortably along the winding road. Overhead the stars glowed and sparkled in a sky that was like black velvet powdered with bluish dust. Flanking a long, stony slope which stretched southward from the road was the belt of desert which barriered the rangeland still farther south. The starlight glinted eerily on weirdly shaped outcroppings of flint and granite and quartz, and the desert was a brooding purple mystery where giant cactuses brandished arms grotesquely malformed and the sands whispered grain upon grain with a sound that was but pin-pricks in the robe of the silence.

Abruptly that robe was ripped by a long, jagged tear of sound. Screaming echoes flung back and forth amid the buttes and chimneys and wailed away to the topmost crags. Again the eerie screech poured through the starlight, and again. Followed a pulsing mutter that grew and grew to a thundering diapson. Slade reined in his horse and stared toward the desert.

Out of the dark rushed a gigantic shape, a single gleaming eye cleaving the shadows with a sword of yellow light, its "body" many-jointed like that of an enormous worm. Rumbling awesomely and shaking the night with the staccato crash of steel on steel, the train roared westward toward where the town of Espantosa was a cluster of murky stars spangled against the background of the hills, a wreath of smoke over the gleaming rails marking its progress.

Thoughtfully, Hatfield followed the bobbing red lights of the caboose until they whisked around a curve and vanished. A little later he also rounded that distant shoulder of the hills and saw the "stars" that were Espantosa. He stiffened slightly as to his ears came a faint popping, like sticks burning in a brisk fire. That sound he knew to be gunshots and he wondered if they signified the exuberance of celebrating cowboys or something of a more sinister nature.

He spoke to the sorrel, and Goldy quickened his pace. Half an hour and he was riding past the railroad yards with its vari-colored lights, its panting engines and clanging freight cars. The town proper lay just a little farther beyond the straggle of shacks that butted up against the yards.

The train had been held at the main lead switch and was just rumbling into the yards.

Under the smoky glare of the yard lights, Hatfield noted the contents of the flats and gondolas. Their unusual cargo puzzled him.

"Building material, steel girders and beams — *not* bridge girders and beams, either — bricks, cut stone," he checked as the cars moved slowly along the lead and onto a yard track. "And some of those box cars, to judge from the dust that's seeped through the cracks, are loaded with cement. Looks like there's going to be some building hereabouts other than railroad building. Funny train load to come into a shack town. Reckon it'll be shoved farther west later."

He brooded about the bustling yard as he rode slowly along the beginning of the unpaved main street of the town.

"Railroad," he mused, half aloud, "railroad. It's progress — just what this country needs — but it's hell, too. Owlhoots follow a railroad like moths after a lantern. This section is in for hell-raising aplenty or I'm a heap mistaken. *The deadline for sheriffs!* And that goes double for Rangers, according to the way of thinking of gents that hang out in this section."

He chuckled a little, his green eyes sunny.

"I've had lots of things thrown at me, feller," he told the sorrel, "includin' hot lead and cold steel and rattlesnakes and rocks,

40

but this is the first time I ever had to dodge trees a hundred feet high and as big around in proportion. Well, that's okay, too, so long as they don't connect, and I reckon it's our business to see they *don't* connect."

The road turned in a wide curve, straightened out and became the main street proper of the construction town. Light began to displace the shadows, raucous noise the pleasant hum and mutter of the yards. The board sidewalks vibrated to the clatter and pound of many feet.

From the open windows and through the swinging doors of saloons came a whirl of voices in a score of keys. The shrill laughter of women mingled with the deep bray of men. The ponderous thump of heavy boots cushioned the sprightly click of dainty high heels. There was a silken swish of short skirts, a slither of cards one upon another, the chink of bottlenecks against glass rims, a pounding of fists upon the "mahogany" as men bellowed for whiskey in uncompromising tones. A miasma-like reek of spilled liquor, stale sawdust, tobacco smoke and sweat thickened the night air. Song, or what passed for it, bellowed forth. There was a whine of fiddles, a tinkle of mandolins, the soft thrum of guitars.

The sprinkling of figures in the street

41

became a jostling crowd as Hatfield progressed. A crowd splashed with color like a drunken rainbow. Cowpunchers with gay shirts and gayer neckerchiefs jostled construction workers in muddy boots and battered hats. The flaming *serapes* of dark-faced Mexicans brushed the red or blue or yellow blankets of saturnine Indians. Here and there a Chinaman with flapping queue, dusky blue blouse, and baggy coolie-pants hustled along hugging a huge bundle.

Once Hatfield noted the shining black features, pouting lips and broad white teeth of a Negro. There were women, too, with eyes brighter than their silks, their lips and cheeks an unnatural red. And the glance of their bright eyes was like the predatory glance of the hawk as he swoops low to survey possible prey. They weaved in and out amid the crowd with swaying hips, tossing curls and self-assurance that was, under the circumstances, slightly disconcerting.

"She's a hell-whooper, all right," the Ranger chuckled, an appropriate name for this sprawling town here in the shadow of the forest and the hills.

The dust of the street was blotched and spotted with raw gold where the light streamed through window and sagging door or chinked through canvas flap or tar-paper

42

covering, and the swirl of motes kicked up by the sorrel's passing hoofs was a cloud of powdered amber. Hatfield narrowed his eyes as he sought for the familiar swinging board sign that would promise quarters for Goldy.

He approached the mouth of a dark alley, glanced along it and saw, outlined in a bar of light, that which he sought.

"Livery Stable," was rudely daubed on a rectangle dangling from wires above a wide doorway a hundred yards or so up the alley.

"Here's where you put on the nosebag, feller," he told the cayuse as he twitched the rein to the left.

Goldy obediently turned, only to be jerked to a sudden halt.

Up the alley had sounded a sullen boom. Hatfield saw a lance of reddish flame split the shadows.

Followed an instant of tingling silence, then a wild pandemonium of yells and shots, and the patter of swift feet running toward the alley mouth.

Hatfield stiffened in the saddle, then swayed sideways in a lightning blur of movement. Buckshot howled through the space his body had occupied the instant before and he felt the hot blast of the charge stir his hair.

Like the flicker of a swooping hawk's wing, he drew with his right hand and snapped a shot under Goldy's neck, the blue smoke trickling in a thin wisp from the rock-steady muzzle of his gun.

There was a yell of agony as the sawed-off shotgun clattered to the ground, the body of its wielder thudding on top of it. Hatfield surged erect, a gun in each hand, as men boiled out the alley mouth.

"Good work, cowboy!" boomed a voice. "You got the murderin' bastard."

Hatfield holstered his guns, swung to the ground and pushed through the crowd gathering about the body.

"What happened?" he asked, squatting beside the dead shotgun artist.

"The skunk dry-gulched a feller through the window of the Sluicegates Saloon," answered a babble of voices. "Blowed him plumb in two with slugs. Nearly got you, too, didn't he?"

Hatfield nodded, his slim hands expertly exploring the body. He turned it over, revealing a dark, contorted face with lank black hair straggling down over the forehead.

"Another Yaqui," he muttered to himself. "What the hell! Has a cage busted?"

He fumbled the pockets of the dead man,

his steely fingers probing deep.

"Don't mess with that body, young feller," said a harsh voice over his shoulder. "I'll take charge of things here."

Hatfield glanced up and saw the speaker was a sturdy old man with a big nickel badge pinned to his sagging vest. He had a square-jawed, weather-beaten face, a straggling moustache and a truculent eye.

"Certainly," Hatfield acquiesced, rising to his feet and deftly palming the object he had drawn from the dry-gulcher's pocket.

Sheriff Nat Rider squinted at him, suspicion in his eyes.

"What the hell's going on here, anyhow?" he demanded.

A half-dozen voices told him, in profane detail. The sheriff's face cleared and he regarded the Ranger with a more favorable glance.

"Good work," Rider said. "These damn half-breeds are gettin' plumb out of hand. Got to be taken down a peg. Glad you did for this hellion, son. Be at my office ten in the mornin' for the inquest. Run over and get my chief deputy, Hawkins, somebody, and I'll go up to the Sluicegates quick as I get this corpse taken care of. You sure poor ol' Cal is dead?"

Hatfield mounted and rode up the street

45

toward the corner which led to the Sluicegates Saloon. Under a bar of light he
glanced at the object still snugged in his
muscular palm. It was a thin metal disk on
which was stamped a number, and letters
which read —

Cibola Timber Co.

Chapter IV

In the Sluicegates Saloon the group about
the slug-riddled body of Cal Hudgins gave
back as the man in the doorway moved
toward them, his feet pounding solidly on
the boards. He was a giant of a man with
enormous shoulders, a barrel of a chest and
a neck like the corded trunk of a fir.

His arms, slightly bent at the elbows, hung
to his knees, and his huge hands, thickly
covered with reddish down, were like poised
spearheads. The face that topped the powerful neck, running to a craggy beak of nose
that dominated the whole, was long of chin
and broad of forehead, with low cheekbones
and thin, tight lips. The close-cropped head
was square and gave an impression of
mental as well as physical toughness.

Despite the iron-gray hair that spoke of
youth left behind, there was an intense viril-

ity about the man. It glowed in his deep-set, cold blue eyes, evinced itself in the set of the square jaw and the lithe swing of the great body as he strode toward the shrinking group, his pace neither fast nor slow.

It was like the inexorable advance of a glacier, that unhurried progress across the big room, a progress that discounted possible obstacles or set them at naught. Inanimate obstructions were to be smashed aside. Animate ones would of necessity make way.

"What about Brush Vane?" he repeated in his rumbling voice.

There was a moment of silence. His erstwhile defamers appeared utterly cowed by the mere presence of Brush Vane. The big cattle and timber baron's long black coat was open and its flowing lines seemed to emphasize the vigor of the man. That open coat also showed a heavy cartridge belt about his lean middle and a big black-stocked gun hanging low on his left thigh, the butt to the front. Vane was evidently a cross-pull man.

The man Vane addressed stared with bulging eyes, his gaze apparently riveted on the length of gold watch-chain strung across the wine-colored vest that served to emphasize the snowy whiteness of shirt front relieved only by the dark thread of a black string tie. He opened his mouth, gulped, swallowed with a convulsive dancing of his prominent Adam's apple.

"Well?" growled Vane, his cold eyes unwavering on the other's face.

The man found his voice. "I — I didn't mean nothing, Mr. Vane," he mouthed thickly. "I was just sayin' —"

"Parsons, don't push a man too far," Vane interrupted menacingly. "This ain't the first time you've sounded off about me. It's come to my ears more than once the things you been saying. I reckon now you been bellowing that I'm responsible for Cal Hudgins being done in? Eh, is that it?"

"I was just sayin' —" Parsons began again despairingly.

The words ended in a terrified squawk as Vane moved with unbelievable swiftness. He covered the remaining distance in a single giant stride, his long right arm with its spearhead hand stabbing out like a lance. Great fingers coiled about Parson's throat, lifted him from the floor and shook him as a terrier shakes a rat. Then Brush Vane held the heavy man at arm's length, his kicking feet clear of the floor, and tightened his mighty grip on his throat.

With frantic hands, Parsons clutched and

tore at the other's wrist, wrenching and prying. He might as well have tried to loosen the grip of a steel cable. His face purpled, his eyes bulged, his tongue protruded from his gaping mouth. His companions shrank back against the wall, white to the lips.

Parson's face was turning black. His feet kicked weakly, his fluttering fingers dropped from Vane's wrist. Vane still held his merciless grip, shaking his helpless victim.

Then, with paralyzing abruptness, other fingers wound about the giant's corded wrist — slim, bronzed fingers that seemed but half the size of Vane's enormous digits. But as Vane whirled about, those slim fingers tightened like rods of nickel steel.

Under that numbing pressure, Vane's hand snapped open, his grip fell away from Parson's throat and the latter sprawled on the floor.

A voice spoke, a softly drawling voice with a hint of steel beneath the velvety tones:

"A little more and you'd done that feller in. Don't figure you wanted to do that, did you?"

Brush Vane goggled in amazement. He glared at the man who had plucked his victim from his grasp, and, tall as he was, he had to raise his gaze a little to meet the level green eyes in the bronzed, impassive face.

For an instant Brush Vane glared, the astonishment leaving his eyes to make way for an expression of black rage. He had not finished with Parsons, not by a damn sight, but first he would take care of this impudent fool who dared to interfere with something Brush Vane was doing.

"Damn you!" he roared, and lashed out with a fist like a sunburned ham.

But before the blow had traveled six inches, it was blocked — blocked with an ease that made Vane appear fumbling and awkward. The green-eyed man weaved aside and, as Vane lunged with the other hand, a fist like the slim, steely face of a sledge-hammer whipped forward and cracked against Vane's jaw.

The unfortunate Parsons, retching and gasping, was just trying to get to his feet when he was knocked flat again by Brush Vane's ponderous body. With a bellow of woe, he flattened out on the floor, his eyes bulging like a stepped-on frog's. Vane, howling curses, tried to scramble erect, tripped on Parson's thrashing legs and sprawled on his nose.

Hatfield, standing with hands on his hips, chuckled at Vane's mishap, his green eyes sunny. Then, like a flicker of lightning on a cloud, the eyes turned coldly gray, and the quiet hands snapped into bewildering action.

Brush Vane had writhed over on his left side and his great right hand had blurred toward the jutting black butt of the heavy Colt holstered against his left thigh. He was indeed a master of the difficult but amazingly fast cross-draw. His hand gripped the black butt and the six flickered from its sheath with a speed the eye could scarce follow.

Crash!

The room shook to a thundering report. Men yelled with apprehension and excitement and dived wildly under tables or behind posts. There was a smashing clatter on the floor boards. Brush Vane roared a mighty curse.

Then he wrung his dripping fingers and glared unbelievingly at the tall figure before him. A little trickle of smoke was wisping up from Slade's right-hand gun. The left-hand one was spinning easily about his forefinger by the trigger guard and the circling muzzle kept men dodging this way and that scrambling for points of safety. Vane's own gun, its lock smashed, its stock splintered, lay yards distant, hurled there by

51

the slug from the Ranger's Colt.

For a long moment Brush Vane propped himself on his elbow and stared at this Lone Wolf. Then he leaped to his feet with the lightness of a boy. Still staring at Hatfield, he nodded, in almost a friendly manner. His anger had apparently evaporated and the object toward which it had originally been directed was utterly forgotten. Said "object" had scuttled under a table on hands and knees and departed via the swinging doors so fast he smoked.

Brush Vane's gaze ran over Hatfield from head to foot — a calculating, all-embracing gaze that missed nothing. He nodded again and his glance became speculative.

"Fast hand, fast eye," he remarked ruminatingly, "may look you over again some time, can't tell."

His deep voice was impersonally conversational. For a third time he nodded. Then he turned, and slowly swept the big room with a cold stare. And under that bleak gaze, men shuffled their feet and glanced nervously aside. Paying not the least attention to the man who had knocked him down and shot a gun from his hand, Vane walked lithely through the swinging doors and vanished.

Instantly the big room roared with comment, much of it profane. Hatfield quietly but firmly pushed his way through a crowd of vociferous admirers to the bar and ordered his own drink despite the offers of a dozen men to buy him one. The bartender poured it with deference, filling the glass to the rim.

"Well, I've seen plenty in my day," he remarked, "but I saw something this night I never expected to — I've seen Brush Vane backwater!"

Hatfield smiled at him over the rim of his glass.

"Wrong, feller," he said, "you still got something to see."

"Eh? How's that?"

"What you saw," Hatfield told him, "was a feller with sense enough not to try to play out a hand in which he didn't hold strong enough cards."

Chapter V

Hatfield had finished his drink and called for another, when a voice spoke at his elbow:

"That was a mighty good chore you did, young man — one that's been needin' doing for quite a spell."

Turning, Hatfield faced the speaker. The Lone Wolf, whose eyes missed nothing, no matter how confused the moment, had seen the man enter the saloon the instant before he shot the gun from Brush Vane's hand. He had been struck by his appearance, and he had later observed him in earnest conversation with other men; evidently getting the low-down on the recent happenings.

He was tall, almost as tall as the Ranger, and slender, with the slenderness, Hatfield thought, of an unsheathed sword. Hair and eyes were tawny, the irises flecked with a darker shade. His face was long and lean, deeply bronzed, his mouth tight above a jutting chin. His slim, wide-shouldered form was close-knit and graceful. His voice, deep, but with a barely perceptible nasal twang.

Hatfield nodded courteous acknowledgment of the other's remark, but did not speak.

The barkeeper came bustling up. "Howdy, Mr. Flint," he greeted heartily, "how's things over to the Texco Lumber camp?"

"About as common, I callate," replied the man addressed as Flint. "I'll take a mite of whiskey-and-water, and fill this gentleman's glass."

"Certain," agreed the barkeep. "Stayin' in town overnight?"

"Don't know but what I be," replied Flint, sipping his watered drink. "Heard they're goin' to hold a town meeting tomorrow to discuss somethin' relatin' to the railrud."

He turned to Hatfield again. "If you're callatin' on stoppin' in this section for a spell, drop in at the Texco camp and see me," he invited. "Might be able to put something in your way."

Hatfield thanked him, and a moment later Flint walked out.

The barkeeper looked after his tall figure admiringly.

"He's a gent, all right," he declared, "but ain't a bit uppity, and don't think he gives the Lord advice about runnin' everything, like Brush Vane figures to do. He's the feller that owns the big Texco Lumber Company up to the north of here. Him and Vane don't get along."

"How's that?" Hatfield asked.

"Well," replied the drink juggler, "two fellers can't be the big skookum he-wolf of a section at the same time. Vane used to be, but since Flint showed up, he ain't had things all his own way. Flint's been coming to the front mighty fast, particular since the railroads began building."

The bartender chuckled a little. "Funny thing," he went on, "Brush Vane really gave Flint his start. Flint came down here from the west Panhandle about two years back and bought a big stretch of timber to the north and west of here. Brush Vane owned all the timber country then, but he sold the biggest part of it to Flint and figured at the time he'd made an almighty shrewd deal. That was before anybody had any idea about the railroads coming this way, and there weren't no market for lumber. Vane held onto the east section of the timber because it had water on it and patches where there was grass his cattle could use, but he let Flint have most of the good pine and oak. Reckon Flint just about sunk his pile in that buy, and everybody hereabouts figured he was plumb loco. Then along come them two railroads racin' each other to the New Mexico mining country and them oil wells up in the northwest, and timber suddenly became almighty valuable. Brush Vane all at once discovered he'd handed a nice fat gold mine to Austin Flint. He ain't liked Flint over well since."

Hatfield grinned at the palpable understatement. The bartender grinned in sympathetic agreement.

"Yeah, Brush sure hates Flint's guts," he chuckled.

"You say Flint came here from up in the Panhandle?" remarked Hatfield. "Where'd he come from before that?"

"No place," replied the bartender. "Born

and raised in that country. I heard him tellin' about it to a bunch of the boys one night. He was raised on a little spread way over close to the New Mexico line. Tried to make the ranch go after his dad died and left it to him, but it's an almighty long drive to markets from there, and a bad one, so he got tired and sold out to a neighbor and drifted south. He sure got a lucky break with that timber buy. Hear he's been dickerin' for a cow spread here of late."

Hatfield gazed at the bartender through slightly narrowed lids. What he had just heard surprised him considerably, but he was careful not to betray his feeling.

"West Panhandle country," he repeated. "Mighty desolate up there."

"Sure is," agreed the drink juggler. "I've heard tell a buzzard has to carry rations when he's makin' a trip across there."

At that moment the sheriff bustled in. He approached the bar and regarded Hatfield with an eye which, while undoubtedly disapproving, held a certain amount of grudging admiration.

"You appear to be keepin' pretty busy since you hit town, young feller," he rasped. "I heard what you did, and I don't want to hear of any more such doin's. Hittin' respectable citizens on the jaw and shootin' hoglegs out of their hands don't go around here. You might have busted one of Brush's fingers."

"If I hadn't stopped him when I did, *he* might have busted a feller's neck," Hatfield replied mildly. "You wouldn't have wanted that to happen, would you, Sheriff?"

Sheriff Nat Rider tugged viciously at his moustache and rumbled something unintelligible in his throat.

"There's too many fellers hereabouts takin' the law in their own hands," he growled.

"Yes, suh, I sure agree with you on that," Hatfield said.

Sheriff Rider regarded him suspiciously, but Hatfield's face showed no hint of guile. The sheriff grunted, nodded surlily to the bartender and strode out.

"You sure had Nat there," chuckled the barkeep, when the sheriff was out of earshot. "Brush Vane is a lot more the law hereabouts than the sheriff's office, and Nat knows it. Nat is honest enough, but Brush Vane got him elected, and naturally beholden to him. Me, I figure Brush ain't such a bad feller as lots of folks say he is, but he's always been the big he-wolf of the section and I reckon he figures whatever he does has to be right because he does it."

Hatfield nodded, and his green eyes were somber. All too often, in the course of his Ranger activities, he had encountered just such a situation. The barons of the open range, their word absolute in the vast territory they controlled, gradually came to consider themselves above all law other than that of their own making.

When the great ranch owner in question was honest and just, that condition had been bearable in the days when his interests were the only interests to be considered; but with the development of the country, with the attendant influx of new settlers, the building of towns and the coming of railroads, ranch interests quickly clashed with the interests of the new arrivals. Then the cattle baron as an administrator of justice did not properly fit into the picture and frequently found himself the sponsor of lawlessness.

Not that they were ready or willing to admit the fact. Nearly all of them resented the coming of strangers — resented the occupation of lands they had come to consider their own, although in most cases their titles were assumed rather than real.

The result was trouble and plenty of it. Here in this raw construction town, Hatfield knew, a situation was developing that was full of dynamite. There had been one murder since he entered the section, and only his own dexterity had prevented a second. He recalled the thundering tree and the creeping dry gulchers with a tightening of his jaw.

"Have one on the house," the bartender invited hospitably.

Hatfield shook his head.

"Got to look after my horse," he said. "Left him at the rack outside."

"Good stable at the head of the alley in back of this dump," suggested the bartender. "Tell Hamhock Harley I sent you. Pretty good feller, Hamhock. Got one eye and a one-track mind, but aside from that he's all right. Uh-huh, he has a room or two over the stalls that he rents to fellers that like to be close to their horses. He'll treat you right."

Hatfield unhitched Goldy and mounted, turning the sorrel's head upstreet.

"Sorry to keep you waitin', feller," he apologized as they turned the corner. "Just figured I ought to take a look at that jigger that got shotgunned, and didn't figure I'd get myself into the middle of a shindig, but that's what happened. And," he added gravely, "it looks like we got ourselves in the middle of something more serious than just a grudge killing. Reckon we're in for a nice trip."

Hamhock Harley appeared close to seven feet tall and about seven inches wide. He gazed sadly at Hatfield from his single eye and shook his head over Goldy.

"The kind of a horse what gets a feller killed sooner or later," he mourned. He ran a bony hand over the sorrel's velvety nose and Goldy nipped playfully at his fingers.

Hatfield's green eyes smiled sunny approval.

"Well, anyway, I'm not scared of losing a cayuse from a feller that can stick his fingers between its teeth," he said.

A truculent expression glowed in Hamhock's eye. "The feller what brings a horse to my stable is the feller what takes him out, unless it's the sheriff what takes 'em both out," he said.

Hatfield nodded. "Give him a good helpin' of oats," he ordered. "He deserves it."

"Right," said Hamhock.

He reached an arm around the side of a stall, gripped a full sack of oats with his enormously long fingers and hoisted it to the height of Goldy's manger without the least apparent effort.

Hatfield's eyes narrowed at this exhibition of strength.

"Seven foot of steel and whipcord," he mused as he started to wash up at the trough.

Hamhock obligingly provided soap and a rough but spotlessly clean towel.

The little room above the stalls was equally rough in furnishings, but just as spotlessly clean as the towel. Hatfield glanced about with satisfaction, combed his thick black hair before a fragment of mirror and descended to the stable again.

"Good eating house down the other end of the alley," Hamhock replied to his question. "Close to the railroad station. Passengers coming in on the night train eat there, so they have good chuck late at night instead of the usual warmed-over slop."

"So they got passenger service here already, eh?"

"Uh-huh, Old Man Dunn of the C & P is a whizzer, he is. He follows his steel with passenger trains as fast as it's laid. Says the way to build a country up is to bring folks into it, and one way to bring them in is to make travellin' easy for 'em. Appears to work, too. Take the L & W town, Preston, to the south of here a dozen miles. There ain't nobody much there besides the fellers what work buildin' the road. Here in Espantosa we got all kinds of folks — almost enough, I figure, to keep the town going even after the railroad building moves on to the west. They're already talking of electin' a regular town government and there's folks what predict the county seat'll be moved here from Vego, where there ain't no railroad."

"Uh-huh, I reckon the road does bring lots of folks in," Hatfield agreed.

Hamhock smiled a rather wry smile. "Not but what we couldn't do without a lot of 'em," he growled. "Can't say as I ever saw such a collection of owlhoots and salty hombres as is got together here of late. And killings are gettin' altogether too frequent. Why, a bastard even shot a horse the other day! Of course, he was shootin' at another jigger, not the horse, but there ain't no excuse for such bad aimin'."

"What'd he do about it?" Hatfield asked, interested.

"He died. The other feller hit what he aimed at."

Hatfield found the restaurant beside the railroad station without trouble. The building was a hastily thrown together affair, like all the others in the town, but an appetizing aroma drifted through its open windows. There also drifted a babble of voices. He climbed the three steps which led to the entrance, opened the door and stepped

63

inside. There was a crashing report and a gun blazed almost in his face.

CHAPTER VI

Hatfield was ten feet along the side wall of the room, a gun in each hand, before he realized that the shot had not been fired at him. The gun wielder, at the moment, was flat on his back on the floor, his smoking weapon knocked from his hand by an angry-faced young man with blue eyes that under normal conditions were undoubtedly pleasant. He was about average height, rather slightly built, but with abnormally long arms that gave him a terrible reach.

The man on the floor was a hulking individual with black whiskers and glittering black eyes. The eyes looked slightly glazed at the moment, however, which attested to the strength of the slim young man's fists. He shook his bushy head from side to side and his heavy face wore an expression of blank amazement that caused Hatfield to chuckle despite the tenseness of the situation.

The melancholy whistle of the incoming passenger train seemed to arouse the prostrate one from his meditations. He mouthed a curse through his beard, shook his head again, and sprang to his feet with catlike agility despite his bulk. He champed his hairy jaws like a wolf as he glared at his smaller opponent, who stood poised and ready, making no move to go for the heavy gun swung low against his left thigh, butt to the front.

"Appears cross-pull men are sort of common hereabouts," Hatfield mused, watching developments with keen interest.

With a roar the bearded man rushed, great arms flailing. The small man stepped lightly aside and hit him — one-two, one-two! Again there was the crash of a falling body, and again the big fellow bounded to his feet, blood dripping from a gashed mouth and a cheek laid open to the bone. Again he rushed, and again the other smashed him in the face.

But this time the bearded man jerked his head aside and the blow was a glancing one. He ducked under the other's fists, and, with a howl of triumph, closed. His thick, knotty arms wound about the smaller man's body and for an instant Hatfield thought it was all over.

But the little man seemed made of steel wires. He successfully resisted the other's efforts to swing him off his feet, bowed his back, locked the heels of his hands under the other's chin. Up and up came the black beard as the young man put forth his strength. From the lips of his opponent spewed a gasping curse. His legs trembled, his straining arms were loosening. He had to let go or suffer a broken neck, and when he did let go he would be at the other's mercy. The younger man grinned thinly, and put on more pressure.

At the same instant Hatfield left the wall like a gigantic spring. In the nick of time his long arm shot out and his fingers gripped the wrist of a man who had crept up behind the battlers.

The knife that had been meant for the slim fighter's back tinkled to the floor. Its wielder, a swarthy, squat individual with high cheekbones and lank black hair, yelled with pain and tried to twist about.

Hatfield let go the wrist and helped him. Then he gripped the knife man by the collar and the seat of the pants and hurled him half across the room. His flying body hit a table of crockery and both he and the table went to the floor in crashing ruin.

The Chinese proprietor of the restaurant screeched profane protest at the destruction. Somebody laughed uproariously. The knife-wielder writhed amid splintered crockery and groaned.

And at that interesting moment the door opened and a girl stepped into the room. Just inside the door she halted, staring in round-eyed amazement tinged with apprehension.

The effect of her entrance was instantaneous and effective. The Chinaman ceased screeching. Men hushed their excited voices. The wrestlers in the center of the room let go their holds and stood back from one another, a sheepish expression on their battered faces. Only the man Hatfield had thrown retained his position, and groaned the louder.

The girl hesitated, gripping the handle of a suitcase with one small hand, apparently uncertain whether to flee. The slim young man was staring at her with his mouth slightly open. His erstwhile opponent had shuffled to one side and was furtively wiping the blood from his face.

Smothering a grin with difficulty, Hatfield stepped forward, bared his black head and smiled down at her from his great height.

"Just a playful wrestling match, Ma'am," he said in his softly drawling voice. "Wasn't expecting ladies at this hour, or it wouldn't have happened."

The girl stared at the groaning knife-wielder, who had been helped to his feet and was being hustled out the back way.

"Playful!" she repeated, her glance flickering to the slim young man.

He had closed his mouth, but not his eyes. Something in their blue depths caused the girl's soft cheeks to color. She glanced hastily away and her gaze sought refuge with the tall Ranger who smiled down at her.

"I'm — I'm hungry," she said. "I've been on the train all day. I expected my uncle to meet me at the station, but he didn't show up. I suppose I can get something to eat here while I wait for him?"

"Certain," smiled the Lone Wolf.

With well concealed amusement, and not a little sympathy, he noted the slim young man edging tentatively in their direction, and there was a twinkling light in his eyes when he spoke.

"I'm sort of busy for a minute, Ma'am," he said, indicating the late battler with a jerk of his thumb, "but I'm sure this gentleman will see you're looked after till your uncle shows up. He's — I declare to goodness, son, your name's plumb slipped me. I'm always forgetting names."

"Vane's the name," the other replied, taking his cue with admirable promptness. "Sheldon Vane. I'll be plumb pleased, Ma'am, to see you get some chuck. Come right over to this big table in the corner!"

The girl's color rose again, but she smiled with her red lips, and also with her eyes, which, Hatfield noted, were the color of ripe tobacco leaves, a color that went well, he thought, with coppery red hair and a creamily tanned complexion with just a suspicion of freckles powdering the bridge of a straight little nose.

"Thank you, Mr. Vane," she said demurely. "I'm Doris Carver, from Dallas. I expect to live with my uncle on his ranch, which I understand is near here."

"What's his brand, Ma'am?" young Vane asked as they turned toward the table.

"It's the Lazy H," the girl replied.

To Hatfield's surprise, the young man halted as if paralyzed, and the Ranger saw the color drain from his face, leaving it a sickly white under the tan. He spoke from stiff lips, his voice barely more than a harsh whisper.

"Your — your uncle, Ma'am — your uncle ain't —"

His voice died before he spoke the name. The girl, wide-eyed with surprise at the sudden agitation of her companion, supplied it.

"My uncle's name is Hudgins," she said, "Calvin Hudgins. Do you know him?"

Chapter VII

To Jim Hatfield fell the unpleasant task of telling Doris Carver that her uncle, Cal Hudgins, had been murdered only a few hours before. Young Sheldon Vane, with a mumbled and incoherent excuse, had fled. Hatfield with understanding, and deep sympathy for his predicament, led the bewildered girl to a table and as gently as possible broke the sad news.

Doris Carver was shocked, and a little frightened, but her reaction was better than Hatfield had hoped for.

"I feel terrible," she told the Ranger, her lips quivering, "but not as I would had I known Uncle Calvin better. I saw him only once when I was a child, and my memory of him is dim. He was my mother's only brother, and when she died more than a year ago, he wrote and urged me to come and live with him. He had never married and I am his only near kin. My father had died several years before and mother was forced to sell our ranch. I had a good job in Dallas, in an office, but I couldn't forget the rangeland — you know how it is."

Hatfield nodded with understanding and the girl continued:

"So I finally decided to take advantage of

Uncle Calvin's offer and come to live with him on the Lazy H. But now — now I don't know what to do."

Her lips trembled, and there were tears in the brown eyes.

Hatfield hastened to divert her from the tragedy.

"The spread's still there, Ma'am," he suggested, "and from what you just told me about being your uncle's only kin, I figure you're owner now. Reckon it's up to you to take charge and straighten things out. Your uncle must have friends and neighbors in this section. Suppose, soon as I get you located in a hotel, I try and round up some of them. They can give you the low-down on things."

"If you only would!" the girl exclaimed gratefully.

"That's settled, then," the Ranger exclaimed heartily. "Now let's surround some chuck. Folks have to eat, no matter what happens, and the way I'm feeling right now, I could gnaw a leg off the table and use the cloth for dessert."

"You're a cowboy, aren't you?" the girl asked, a little later.

"When I'm working at it, I am," Hatfield replied. She took the meaning he intended her to, and in the conversation that followed, showed a thorough familiarity with range work.

"You'll make out," Hatfield told her approvingly. "Now let's see if we can rustle you a place to pound your ear for the night. That's next in order, I reckon. No, I don't think you should go to see your uncle's body tonight. Wait until morning. Everything's being done for him that can be done."

"I wonder what was the matter with that nice Mr. Vane?" said the girl as they arose to go. "Why did he run off like that?"

"I reckon he was worried about what happened," Hatfield replied evasively. "Chances are he went to lock up some of your uncle's friends."

The Ranger had gathered enough from scraps of conversation overheard in the saloon to enable him to appreciate the predicament in which Sheldon Vane had suddenly found himself. Vane had undoubtedly been very favorably impressed by Doris Carver. Just one of those things that happen to a man and in a few short moments make of him something decidedly different from the carefree individual he was before it happened.

That Sheldon Vane was doubtless the son of Brush Vane, the cattle baron, he surmised, and this being so, the younger Vane must be aware of what was being said of his father relative to Cal Hudgins' death. And he would realize that very quickly, Doris Carver would also hear those things, and react accordingly. Acting on a hunch, Hatfield asked a casual question as he paid the bill —

"What was the fight between those two fellows over?"

"Feller Missur Vane knock down all same work for Missur Austin Flint," replied the Chinese proprietor. "He say Missur Vane father have man all same shot. Missur Vane he hit."

"So I noticed," Hatfield agreed dryly.

After seeing to it that the girl had the best accommodations the ramshackle hotel could provide, he rounded up, with the help of Hamhock Harley, a couple of elderly cattle men who had long been friends of Cal Hudgins, and acquainted them with the latest developments.

"We'll see she's looked after proper," they assured Hatfield.

"We've already arranged everything to be done for poor ol' Cal. Thanks for tellin' us, feller, and leave it to us."

Hatfield went to bed, but although it was long past midnight, he did not immediately go to sleep. So many stirring happenings had been packed into the hours since sunset that it seemed that days instead of hours had passed since he took the short cut through the woodland of the Cibola Timber Company. Fingering the two metal discs he had taken from the bodies of the dry-gulchers, he thought of Captain McDowell's parting words —

"It looks like an open-and-shut case what had ought to be handled by the local authorities," Cap. Bill had said when he ordered his ace man to ride the seventy-odd miles to Espantosa, and investigate the series of killings which had stirred the section.

"There's always trouble when new forces come into a district," Captain McDowell went on. "Usually it's just the regulation fightings and shootings, and all you got to do to handle the situation is grab the gunslingers and jug 'em; but sometimes it don't work that way. Recollect what happened when they were building the railroad over in the salt desert country. That looked like an open-and-shut case, too, at first, but you sure found it something a heap different before you got through with it.

"Better amble over to Espantosa. Folks over there are yelling for a troop, but I'd like to know where the hell I'm going to get a troop to spare right now. Been ordered to send every available man to the Border. Look things over, Jim, and straighten 'em out." One brief remark of McDowell's had impressed Hatfield. "Folks over there seem scared," Captain Bill had said.

Hatfield knew that the people who lived in the country between the Nueces and the Border were not the sort to scare easily. Nor would an ordinary row between rival interests, be those interests cattle, lumber or railroad, do little more than intrigue or irritate them.

During the trip to Espantosa, he had suspected that there was much more to the situation than what appeared on the surface. The happenings since he arrived in the vicinity of the construction town had confirmed his suspicion. Stealthy, vicious murder — dry-gulching from the dark — was something to shake the nerves of the boldest. And it was something the honest but fumbling old sheriff was doubtless unequipped to cope with. Nat Rider might do fine work running down rustlers or jugging tough gunmen, but here was a manifestation of subtle, crafty and utterly ruthless forces working to some unknown ends.

That the situation might be pregnant with

deadly danger for himself was something to which Hatfield gave little thought.

That he was in danger, even he might have admitted could he have overheard the conversation taking place at that very moment in the dingy back room of a villainous little saloon near the edge of the Mexican quarter of the town.

Two men sat at a table. The flickering light from a smoky oil lamp illumined the face of one, a fat man with a face too small for his massive body. He had hard little eyes that caught the light like agates. His jaw was long and powerful, but his mouth was just loose enough to, at times, reveal a glimpse of stubby, crooked teeth. He had a habit of rubbing the sharp bridge of his nose with a plump hand.

The second man sat with his back to the light, his hat brim pulled low over his face, his powerful shoulders hunched forward.

"I don't know who the hell he is, but I do know he did for Miguel," he was saying.

"Miguel killed Hudgins first, didn't he?" interpolated the fat man.

"Uh-huh, and would have got in the clear if it hadn't been for that seven-foot hellion with his chain-lightnin' draw. Anyhow, he drilled Miguel dead center which was a good thing. Miguel didn't have a chance for any deathbed confessions."

"I wonder if killing Hudgins wasn't a mistake," said the fat man. "I still believe I could have talked him into selling out."

"Like hell you could," snarled the other. "He was stubborn as a blue-nosed mule. He was born and raised on that spread and figured on dyin' there. Trying to make him sell was just like tryin' to freeze him out by taking his cattle market with the railroad away from him. *That* didn't work, either; just got him on the prod and made him stubborner than ever. I tell you, killing him was the only way."

"Well, you know people here better than I do," admitted the fat man. "But about this man who killed Miguel — you haven't learned who he is or where he came from?"

"No. He looks like a range tramp — a cowhand that drifts from one job to another and don't settle down nowhere — and he looks like an owlhoot, and sure handles his gun like one. What I don't like to think is that maybe he's some smart gunfighter folks around here have hired to come up and straighten things out. Judgin' from what he did in the Sluicegates Saloon, he might be anything."

The speaker rubbed his jaw reminiscently as he uttered the words.

"We can't have any interference at this stage of the game," declared the fat man. "I used every bit of political pull I had to get that Ranger company of McDowell's sent to the Border to keep watch on an uprising that isn't going to take place. A troop of Rangers sent over here right now might easily have proved fatal to our plans. Rangers have a habit of seeing things other people miss."

"Yeah, damn 'em!" growled the other. "We certainly don't need no Rangers here."

"About that big gunman," began the fat man, when a soft tapping at the outer door interrupted him.

His companion's right hand dropped swiftly beneath the table top.

Again the tapping came, evenly spaced, insistent.

"That's the signal," he muttered. "Let 'em in — but step back from the door when you open it."

He sat rigid while the other crossed the room, and his intent gaze never left the rectangle of the door jambs.

Swiftly the fat man slipped a bolt and drew the door open, stepping back behind its rough, thick boards as he did so.

The man at the table tensed and his right hand moved slightly. Then he grunted and relaxed as two swarthy, furtive-eyed men glided into the room, closing and bolting the door behind them.

"Well?" the man at the table questioned harshly.

"Tree fall," grunted the foremost of the newcomers.

"The hell you say! Was *he* under it?"

The speaker swore a Spanish oath and his beady eye flashed resentfully.

"No under — nobody under," he replied. "We hear tree fall — go see — go all same snake in brush. See nothing — hear nothing. Sudden come gun shoots. Estaban die — Pedro die."

The seated man surged to his feet, crashing his chair to the floor behind him. From his great height he glowered at the speaker, his hand twitching to his gun butt.

"You mean to say that hellion was there waitin' for you and gunned you?" he spat.

The other's dark eyes flickered, but he sturdily held his ground.

"No see," he intoned monotonously. "No see nobody. See *caballo dorado*."

"A golden horse!" translated the tall man. "You mean a sorrel! *He* don't ride no sorrel. He was ridin' a black today."

"See *caballo dorado*," the swarthy man droned.

The other glared at him. Then suddenly with a rasping curse he swung toward the fat man, who was standing rubbing the bridge of his nose and nervously shifting his feet.

"A sorrel!" he repeated, his voice cracking high with rage. "That gunslinger was ridin' a sorrel — the finest lookin' horse I ever saw."

He whirled back to the news bearer.

"You say he did for Estaban and Pedro? Why the hell didn't you two do for *him?* Four against one!"

The other turned his head to show a raggedly furrowed cheek.

"No see — feel!" he grunted. "Come 'way fast, 'fore go like Pedro and Estaban."

The tall man glared, speechless, but making incoherent noises in his throat. Then suddenly his voice became level again, his tones cold and calculating.

"This settles it," he said to the fat man. "That feller, whoever he is, has got to be taken care of. Don't know who he is, or what he knows, but we're takin' no chances."

There was a quality in the quiet voice that caused the fat man to turn his eyes aside and wet his suddenly dry lips with a nervous tongue.

The other righted his fallen chair and sat down again. For some minutes he stared straight in front of him, his face a formless blob in the shadow. Then he beckoned the two swarthy men, and spoke to them at length. And as he unfolded his plan, their eyes glittered with evil anticipation. But the fat man's face, as he heard that sentence of death pronounced, and the manner of its execution, blanched to a pasty gray, and as the speaker sat back with a satisfied bearing, he breathed between stiff lips —

"God!"

CHAPTER VIII

The coroner's inquest the following morning was brief and informal, the verdict typical of cow country juries. It read:

Cal Hudgins was murdered by a dry-gulching hellion who got what was coming to him pronto.

Several members of the jury made it a point to shake hands with Hatfield, after hearing his corroborated testimony tell how the half-breed killer came to death.

"And now let's ev'body hustle down to the railroad depot," said Sheriff Rider. "Old

Man Dunn has somethin' to say, I understand."

Hatfield spoke to Doris Carver, who sat, pale but composed, through the hearing.

"We're taking Uncle Calvin's body to the ranch for burial," she told the Ranger. "Mr. Bush and Mr. Gerard here have been so kind. They have arranged everything."

The two grizzled cowmen looked as embarrassed as if they had been caught in some reprehensible act.

"Wasn't nothin'," Bush said awkwardly, "nothin' what wouldn't be expected of a neighbor."

"I'm havin' my Missus go over to the Lazy H and see the little lady gets settled okay," put in Gerard. "I sent word to the Lazy H boys last night and I'll have a talk with 'em when they ride in this morning."

Hatfield smiled down at the two oldsters and there was a warm light in his strangely-colored eyes, and his usually stern face was singularly pleasant. He shook hands with each before leaving.

"Real," he said to himself as he forked Goldy and rode toward the station, where a crowd was quickly gathering. "Real folks — the kind this country needs, and the kind whoever's raising hell in this section is hitting at."

His face grew stern at the thought, but his green eyes quickly became sunny again.

"And the chance to make things a little easier for real folks like that makes a peace officer's work worth while," he murmured softly.

Doris Carver followed his tall form with her eyes until it vanished from view.

"The kind of a horse a feller dreams about but never expects to see," remarked lanky old Bush, about the sorrel.

"And the kind of a *man* a girl dreams about — and never gets," said Doris.

Bush glanced at her with a startled expression. Then a thought seemed to strike him and he slapped his thigh.

"That big feller ain't tied up with no outfit, is he?" he asked of fat, comfortable looking Sam Gerard.

"Don't reckon he is, Mack," replied Gerard. "Appears from what he said he's just passin' through, sort of on the lookout for anything what'd offer."

"Hmmm!" said Bush, "hmmm!" But he made no further comment.

A rough platform had been hastily thrown together fronting the open space beside the flimsy depot. Here the crowd gathered wearing an air of anticipation. There was a murmur, then silence, when a man came from the depot, mounted the steps to the platform and stood gazing over the throng of upturned faces.

He was a big old man, heavily built, with an enormous spread of shoulders, abnormally long arms and powerful hands. His eyes were frosty blue, his mouth tight but kindly, his nose prominent below the big dome of a forehead from which swept back a glorious crinkly mane, snow white.

It was James G. Dunn, affectionately known as "Jaggers" to the thousands of husky railroaders who swore by him, though they might swear at him — when Jaggers was out of hearing. This was Jaggers Dunn, ex-cowboy, ex-soldier of fortune, ex-engineer, empire-builder, General Manager of the great C & P railroad system.

Dunn's all-embracing glance swept the crowd and his blue eyes paused for a moment where the tall Ranger sat his magnificent horse on the outskirts of the crowd — paused for an instant, then moved on without a hint of recognition.

Hatfield chuckled. He had counted on Jaggers Dunn's intuition and innate caution, and Dunn had not failed him.

The General Manager spoke, and his words were brief and to the point.

"I have an announcement to make," he said without preamble. "As you all know, this town was built with only temporary occupancy in mind. It was built primarily to accommodate the thousands of C & P construction workers. With the extension of railhead to the west, these workers must of necessity, a large majority of them, at least, be moved westward so as to be nearer the scene of active operations."

He paused, and a murmur ran through the crowd which had just listened to the death sentence of Espantosa. Then came the reprieve.

"However," said Dunn, "I have for some time been studying the strategic location of Espantosa and have been considering the fact that it forms the natural focus of the extensive timber and ranching operations of the district. There is also a hint of possible mineral deposits in the Espantosa Hills to the north and west. This last is, of course, based only on supposition. But based only on supposition were the oil deposits of the Alamita Basin and the silver of the Tamarra Hills — until discovery made of them a valuable reality.

"In consequence, with these things in mind, I have decided that Espantosa shall become a permanent settlement, and a division point for the C & P line now building. Extensive shops, roundhouses and yards will be constructed here, and division offices for the road. Last night the first trainload of materials for the new construction rolled into the Espantosa yards. It will be quickly followed by others."

He turned and walked toward the platform steps, his feet pounding solidly on the boards, and in that measured, unhurried, positive stride, Jim Hatfield saw typified the new forces that were stirring themselves here in the wild border country of the Nueces. Jaggers Dunn was the first herald of these forces of progress and development, just as he himself was the spear-point of the new force of law and order that must keep pace with the swift advance of material things that would bring a wave of chaos into the vacuum behind its too-speedy progress.

"Yeah, we got our work cut out for us, feller," he told the sorrel. And his green eyes held a light of pleasant anticipation.

He rode slowly through the cheering crowd, reached the livery stable and turned Goldy over to Hamhock Harley. Then he sauntered to the railroad yards and wandered aimlessly along the tracks.

Or at least his progress would have appeared aimless to anyone observing it. He

86

paused to glance at loaded freight cars, examined switch stands, watched the work of switching crews with absorbed interest, and in other ways played the part of an idle cowhand intrigued with the mysteries of railroading.

Presently, he reached a quieter sector of the yard. Here no engines puffed and hissed, no cars were shuttled back and forth in apparently purposeless confusion. A moment later, he paused beside a long green-and-gold splendor with *Winona* stencilled in gold leaf on the sides. He walked swiftly to the rear of the private car, glanced around, and swung up the steps to the observation platform. Without the formality of knocking he pushed open the door and entered.

There was a frightened squawk and an aged Negro, his eyes rolling white in his shining black face, scuttled frantically toward an inner compartment.

"Mistuh Dunn! Mistuh Dunn!" he yammered. "Heah comes ol' Jesse James hisself to pistol-shoot us all!"

"Shut up, George, and get the hell out of here," rumbled a deep voice. "Come in, Hatfield."

His green eyes glowing with amusement, and not the least surprised that Jaggers Dunn should have instantly surmised the identity of his visitor, Hatfield crossed to the inner door and entered the presence of the empire-builder. The old porter whizzed through a further door, his eyes still rolling with apprehension, and vanished in the direction of the kitchen. Jaggers Dunn stood up behind his big desk, reached a huge paw across it and shook hands warmly.

"Been two years, hasn't it, since we last met?"

Hatfield nodded. He envisioned that last meeting, amid flaming guns, when hordes of outraged and exploited people raved for blood and vengeance — a vengeance denied only by the Lone Wolf's iron courage and the driving force of a personality that set odds at naught.

Jaggers Dunn smiled a little to himself as he recalled the tall figure of the Ranger riding into the sunset, his lithe form etched in flame. He had ridden away to new adventures where death lurked, to put his keen brain and his unerring guns against the ruthless enemies of law and order, and the empire-builder, conning the stacks of dry-as-dust detail that cluttered his desk, had often thought of the man who had been his friend, and who had saved his life at the risk of his own.

No, Jaggers Dunn did not forget.

"I figured you'd be dropping in when I saw you this morning," he said. "McDowell sent you over? I understand people here asked for a troop. They're lucky at that, only they don't know it. You're in luck, too, Hatfield, judging from the pleasure you get out of situations that would drive most folks to nervous prostration. There's something building up here that's liable to give even you a bellyful."

"Trouble?" asked the Lone Wolf.

"Trouble's a mild word for it," growled Dunn. "I'm used to trouble when building railroads, and to competition that doesn't choose its weapons with delicacy, and even to fairly-sized wars, but the things that have happened here make even what I've been used to, mild."

He paused, and Hatfield took the chair he indicated. The General Manager opened a drawer of his desk, fumbled for a minute and drew forth something wrapped in silk cloth.

"A sample," he said, laying the object at Hatfield's elbow.

Wondering, the Ranger unwound the silk. Then he started back with an exclamation and stared at the thing lying on the shining top of the desk. It was a human hand, severed at the wrist, the flesh withered and smoke-blackened.

Chapter IX

Hatfield raised his gaze to Jaggers Dunn and his eyes asked a question.

"Belonged to one of our best railroad detectives," Dunn said, a cold glitter in his blue eyes. "A man I had sent out here to investigate the killings along our construction line. He came back to camp one night, tied to his horse, what was left of him — the horse brought his body to camp — with this thing dangling around his neck by a buckskin thong."

"And it came from —"

"Came from his right arm. It had been chopped off with an ax or a big knife. The stump had been plunged into hot coals to sear the severed arteries and stop the bleeding. Must have lived quite a while after it was done, and his tongue cut out. Another man, the first fellow's brother, took over the job. Swore he'd track down his brother's killers and avenge him. He'd had considerable experience in the West, like his brother, and was at home in the hills."

"And?"

"He didn't come back, and I'm not going

to show you what did. I had it decently buried."

"What was it?"

"His head! His head, minus the eyes and the tongue. The tongue had been torn out, apparently gripped with a big pair of pincers and ripped from his jaws. The eyes had been burned out."

"Done while the man was still alive?"

"Judging from the tortured expression on the face, I'd say yes."

"Any idea where all this was done?"

"We backtracked them into the mouth of Espantosa Canyon. What they were doing way up there, hell only knows. It's two miles north of the right-of-way, and twenty west of where railhead was at the time. We're closer, now!"

"Looks like one of them might have stumbled on something," Hatfield said.

"Uh-huh," Dunn replied, "something that tripped them!"

"What happened next?" Hatfield asked.

"Well," said Dunn with a wry smile, "there has been a bit of a strike among our railroad police. You can't pry one of them away from the steel with a crowbar. They patrol the line of the rails, but they don't go out of sight of 'em."

Hatfield nodded sympathetic understanding. He could well understand the feelings of the railroad police, most of them city men who were lost and bewildered in this wild land of great distances, weird natural formations and savage instincts. Brave enough they might be, in familiar surroundings, but here they suffered the terror of the unknown, than which there is no worse fear. The gruesome fate of their unfortunate fellows had numbed them with dread and peopled the hill and desert country with grim spectres born partly from their own fevered imagination, but terribly real to them, nevertheless. No, this was certainly not a job for railroad bulls. The Lone Wolf's face was bleak as he carefully examined the withered hand.

"Yaqui work," he said at length. "They smoke members this way, and ornament the walls of their cabins with them.

"But," he added with meaning, "hanging the smoked hand around the neck of the man it belonged to and then sending him riding back where he came from is *not* Yaqui work."

"Eh!" exclaimed Dunn, "what do you mean?"

"I mean," Hatfield replied quietly, "that although doubtless it was Yaqui Indians from down below the Line that cut off that poor devil's hand and smoked it, it was a white man or men who hung it around his neck, tied his body to the horse and sent him back where he came from as a warning to others. No Yaqui would ever have done that. Yaquis wouldn't have stopped at cutting off his hand if they'd caught him and were torturing him.

"They'd have done more, plenty more. And sending back the head of a feller they'd tortured to death would be clean outside Yaqui understanding. No, that part of the job was white man's work. Done to strike terror in others."

He paused and regarded the empire-builder, who was rumbling profanity in his throat.

"And now, suh, can you tell me anything as to what this is all about?"

Dunn hesitated a moment, stroking his big chin with his hand.

"I can tell you something, but not all," he said at length. "A lot of what has been going on here is beyond my understanding. When I started building this line, I expected bitter competition — the competition of an able, ambitious man into whose path fate has thrown opportunity and who is determined to make the most of it, and not at all particular as to what means he uses to achieve his end. But I did not expect the things that have happened in this section. We have had camps burned, railroad lines destroyed, material trains wrecked, and have suffered similar depredations.

"All this was to be expected — I have experienced such things before, and will not be surprised to experience them again — but the killings and torturings, the stealthy murders, the night attacks by cunning marauders who appear from nowhere and vanish into the darkness when their work is done, those are things I did not expect even from the man now at the head of the L & W system. And I still cannot see him as responsible for them.

"I don't credit Bijah Cosgrove with a shrinking delicacy or qualms of conscience that would cause him to hesitate at much, but it is not his way, nor his methods. As I see it, such means just naturally wouldn't occur to him. I have come to the conclusion that other and more sinister forces are operating here and are prepared to go to any lengths to prevent the building of the C & P railroad through this section."

"Who and what is Cosgrove?" Hatfield asked.

"He's president and construction manager of the L & W railroad," Dunn replied. "He used to be a ward-heeler, a minor politician in New York. Brought up and educated in a hard school. Lived a rough-and-tumble life in the city during his early years. Was in with the political machine there and never amounted to much. Managed to get in jail a few times — nothing serious. Fighting, minor shootings, election rows — but never served much time and never went to state prison. The kind of things expected of a young political thug in those days, and nobody thought any the less of him because of them. Seems he got tired of the life, though, or had a falling out with some of the higher-ups, perhaps.

"Anyway, he went to work for a railroad and there he showed real ability. Finally he drifted south and tied up with the L & W. That road was just a very lengthy streak of rust in those days, and getting rustier as the years passed. Finally its stock dropped to almost nothing, and through shrewd manipulation and by interesting some local capital, Cosgrove got control."

"And sort of changed things?"

"He certainly did. He galvanized that old skeleton into particularly lively life. The first thing the railroad world knew, the L & W was one of the leading southern lines, and reaching out for new territory. Of L & W methods, the least said the better, but Cosgrove certainly got results."

"And then?"

"And then when I conceived the idea of this new C & P line to the oil and mining fields and the southwest cattle country that is badly in need of efficient transportation, I learned that Cosgrove was right there with the same idea."

Hatfield chuckled, and Dunn grinned wryly.

"Yes," he continued, "Cosgrove was right there. Now, as the situation stands, there are contracts involving millions of dollars hanging in the air and waiting the outcome of this race between the C & P and the L & W. And that's to say nothing of extensive mail contracts that are a particularly fat and juicy plum for any railroad."

"And if Cosgrove beats you to the objective?"

Jaggers Dunn shrugged his big shoulders. "Then," he said grimly, "I will have a thousand-odd miles of unproductive railroad on my hands. Which will mean dropping of C & P stock values, lower dividends, and trouble with the Board of Directors and the stockholders and explanations to make that won't explain. Also, it will mean heavy, in some instances, crippling losses for local ranchers and farmers who have invested in the project. It is a C & P custom, you know, to always interest local capital and give the residents a chance to share in the road's profits. They keep us in business, and I feel they should be part of the business. That angle worries me most of all."

Hatfield nodded and his lean face was serious. He fully understood Dunn's predicament. Also, he understood something else, something that he considered far more vital than the difficulties which would beset the empire-builder. Dunn had weathered such storms before, and would weather this one. To the great C & P system, this new line was but an incident. Its profits, if it were successfully completed, would merely go to swell the already comfortable income of the trunk line. If it were forced to operate at a loss, or, which was more likely, to abandon the project, the C & P would absorb the loss and not feel it.

But to the Southwest country and its people, the new C & P line would be as an artery of clean, fresh, life-giving blood. It would rejuvenate the vast land of the Nueces, make conditions far better for the people who lived here, bring law and order into a section that bitterly needed both. Hatfield was familiar enough with Dunn's management of his great railroad to know that the coming of the C & P road would be an undisguised blessing to the community. The L & W was a different matter. He knew that Jaggers Dunn had outlined L & W conditions, management and business methods without rancor or prejudice. He could rely on what Dunn said. The L & W, while bringing needed transportation to the country, would be a decidedly mixed blessing.

Hatfield had had some experience with unscrupulous railroad rules and knew what it meant. And first and foremost his thoughts were with the people of his state, of this lusty land of big things that he loved — this land which was ready and glad to shelter in its fertile arms untold thousands who would come seeking the opportunity for happiness and fuller life.

Jim Hatfield was proud of his state, proud of the part he had played to make it a better place in which to live, confident of its future, and imbued with a burning desire to make it and keep it a worthy, respected and admired part of his native land.

Jaggers Dunn was speaking again.

"You have some idea, now, of what is going on," he said. "As I mentioned before, some of these things were to be expected.

Others I cannot understand, and I am loath to lay them at Bije Cosgrove's door. What do you think, Hatfield?"

The Lone Wolf turned in his chair and pointed through the open window. Far to the west and north was the gaunt loom of the Espantosa Hills, fanging up into the blue of the Texas sky, their ragged battlements glittering in the hot sunshine, their mighty shoulders purple and blue and depressing mauve. Here and there their ominous wall was slashed with the dark mouths of canyons and gorges. Dry water courses scored their sides. At their feet the desert rolled in a shimmering wave of molten gold.

"People live up there," the Lone Wolf said. "People who don't want railroads, or progress. Their kind has always lived there. Centuries ago it was the Lipans or the Apaches. Maybe before that the Yaquis, who later moved south of the Border. They were bad in those days, just as they're bad now. They preyed on the peaceful, progressive Aztecs, and those who went before them. Then, as now, this country was the gateway to the North. Later, after the Apaches and Lips, came the Comanches. And all the time this section remained the gateway from Mexico to the North. Right now the pack

99

trains are amblin' across the prairie and the desert, and right now the raiders from the Espantosa Hills are on the lookout for them.

"Those folks don't want a railroad. They know if one comes, Law will come with it. They'll fight it to the bitter end, just as they fought the stage lines. The southern branch of the Overland Company tried to establish a line through the Nueces country, and failed up. The outlaws of the Espantosa Hills beat them back. The old Overland Line runs to the north of the Espantosa Hills and curves around their western tip to get to the southwest country."

Jaggers Dunn swore harshly. "Those hellions aren't to be allowed to clog the wheels of progress," he declared.

"No," Hatfield agreed grimly, "but they're sure out to poke a stick between the spokes.

"I bet," he added shrewdly, "that the L & W hasn't had half the trouble you have. Those jiggers recognize the different methods of the two roads, and if they have to have a railroad, they'd a whole lot rather have one like the L & W, run by folks that'll wink at their doings just so they let the road alone."

"You're right about that," Dunn agreed. "Also there is something else to consider, if your deductions are correct. The L & W line of survey swerves just west of here and passes many miles to the south of the hills, on the other side of the desert, to be exact. That may make a decided difference."

"It would," Hatfield replied grimly. "Looks to me, suh, like you and I are in for a lively time of it."

Dunn nodded, and for some time Ranger and railroad magnate sat silent, each busy with his own thoughts. It was quiet in the private car. The hum and mutter of the busy yards drifted from the distance in a monotonous and soothing undertone. In the kitchen of the private car, the old Negro who was Dunn's combination porter-chef, chanted in a sweet, low voice that was barely audible where they sat.

Hatfield's gaze drifted out the window and rested on the dense thickets that clothed the crest of the steep bank beyond the yards. Absently his keen glance noted a blur of stealthy movement amid the growth. "Some little critter," his busy mind catalogued the tiny swirl of leaves. He did not realize that the bank overlooked the whole yard, and was unaware that from the concealment of the growth, beady black eyes had watched his every move since he entered the yards. He had not seen those eyes burn with a sudden interest as he reached the private car. A

101

moment later they had vanished from the fringe of the growth as their lithe owner made his stealthy way through the chaparral.

Jaggers Dunn was busy writing something on a sheet of paper. Hatfield still sat deep in thought. Suddenly his dark head flung up in an attitude of listening. His keen ears had caught what sounded like a choking gurgle. He listened intently, heard nothing more, and relaxed. It was doubtless water sputtering through a drain pipe in the kitchen, or a seeping of air from the brake drum beneath the car. The explanation was obvious.

But for so long had the Lone Wolf ridden with deadly danger as his saddle companion, that there was in him developed to an uncanny degree a sixth sense that warned of danger when, apparently, no threat was present. And even now that unseen, unheard monitor was clamoring for attention.

Hatfield glanced wonderingly about. He had learned never to disregard that uncanny prompting. But what could threaten him with harm here in this comfortable setting. The old empire-builder still wrote industriously at his desk. The warm sunshine streamed through the open windows, staining the soft greens of the upholstering with gold. A little breeze fanned the thick black

102

hair at his bronzed temples. Everything was sunshine and peace. But still that silent voice clamored for attention.

Abruptly Hatfield realized that something was missing. At first he was at a loss to define it. Then he suddenly recalled that he had not heard the Negro's chant for some moments. He strained his ears, bending his head in the direction of the kitchen. All was silence there. No, not quite. To his ears came a faint, monotonous hissing, like to the hissing of an angry snake under a distant bush. It was a sound that did not belong in this setting, that was as utterly alien to it as would have been the presence of the snake itself. Still it persisted, barely audible, but in some undefinable way, ominously threatening.

Jim Hatfield crossed the compartment in a single bound. Dunn's pen clattered on the desk as he flung up his head in astonishment. The Lone Wolf strode through the sleeping compartment, the tiny dining room, flung open a door that stood slightly ajar, and the kitchen was before him.

On the floor lay the body of the old porter, his face contorted, blood seeping from a gash in his wooly scalp. And beside him, hissing and sputtering and throwing off a train of pale yellow sparks, was a bundle of

103

greasy sticks tied firmly together. And from the end of one of the dynamite sticks protruded the burning fuse. The shower of sparks was all but lapping the head of the detonating cap.

CHAPTER X

Hatfield lunged for the bundle of dynamite, reaching into his pocket for his knife the same instant. He swore a bitter oath as he recalled lending the knife to Hamhock Harley and not having it returned. His gaze swept the little compartment as he scooped the dynamite from the floor. There should be knives aplenty in a kitchen.

Perhaps there were, but the old chef was an orderly soul and had them safely put away in some drawer or cubby-hole, and there was no time to rummage through drawers in search of them. Hatfield gripped the fuse with his teeth and gnawed frantically.

He felt the tough fibre give. Another strand parted, and another. He gasped with pain as a shower of stinging sparks seared the roof of his mouth. Already the fire was washing the cap. He could not hope to bite the fuse off short enough.

Gripping the hissing bundle of death with

his right hand, he lunged for the outer door, which stood slightly ajar.

There was a slamming crash as his big shoulder hit the door, snapping it back on its hinges. He reached the front vestibule, drew back his hand and hurled the dynamite with all his strength.

The hissing bundle cleared a string of box cars two tracks distant and described a long parabola toward the growth fringing the top of the bank. In mid-air it exploded.

Stunned, deafened, his eyes blinded by the yellow glare of flame that paled the morning sunlight, Hatfield was swept to the floor by the howling blast of displaced air. All about him, thudding on the roof, smashing the windows, rasping along the sides of the coach, hurtled stones and earth and fragments of wood and steel.

The private car rocked and swayed on its springs. Every pane of glass was shattered, the doors were jammed on their hinges. A hot water tank burst and swirling clouds of steam filled the compartments. Through the pandemonium wailed the terrified screeches of the old chef, who had recovered consciousness and was grovelling on his kitchen floor.

Jaggers Dunn was roaring profanity and groping his way through the steam. He fell over the scuffling body of the chef, and measured his ponderous length on the floor. Old George bawled the louder and Dunn accomplished new and bewildering feats of profanity. A moment later he pounded out of the steam onto the platform, dragging the squalling chef by the collar.

Hatfield was just getting to his feet. He could see Dunn's lips moving, but the pounding in his ear drums jumbled the G.M.'s words to an incoherent jargon. Waves of fire still blazed before his eyes and it was several moments before he could resume command of his disordered faculties.

Men were running across the yard, yelling questions. They halted to stare in amazement at the yawning crater torn in the steep bank which walled the yard, and the havoc adjoining it. Two boxcars had been derailed and a third was smashed and splintered. The private coach looked like it had undergone an artillery bombardment. Old George was still bleeding from the cut on his head and Jaggers had a gash over one eye where his skull had met a window ledge with stunning force. Hatfield had a burned mouth, but otherwise was intact.

Jaggers Dunn quickly quieted the rumpus and brought order from chaos. He sent men to scour the brush atop the bank, directed others to repair the damage done to his private coach, sent for the wrecker to handle the derailed cars. There was a medical kit in the coach and Hatfield was already cleansing and bandaging the gash on the darky's head. Jaggers plastered his own slight cut, refusing the Ranger's aid.

Hatfield drew Dunn and the old porter to one side, out of earshot of the excited and gabbling workers.

"What happened, George?" he demanded.

The porter scuffed his wooly head with a still shaking hand.

"I hear somebody make steps outside," he replied. "I turn around and man step in door. I start say, 'How come you in Mistuh Dunn's car?' But 'fore I get my mouf open he bang me on head with the barrel of a pistol-gun long as a cross-tie and most as big around. I see stars and comets and whirligigs. Dat's the last thing I know till sky bust open and come fallin' down."

"You got a look at the feller that slammed you?" Hatfield asked.

"Uh-huh, berry good look. Little mean lookin' feller with snake eyes and black hair hangin' down over 'em — feller 'most as black as me only not shiny."

"His hair was hanging down over his

forehead, cut sort of square across?"

"Yassuh! Yassuh! Dat was it. Look like he hab no mouf 'tall — jest cut place 'cross his face. Look like ol' debbil — mebbe he was."

"You ain't missing it over much, George," Hatfield told him grimly. He turned to Jaggers Dunn.

"Judging from George's description, my guess is the hellion was a Yaqui. Appears there's a cage of 'em busted in this section."

"I've seen quite a few around here," Dunn said thoughtfully.

"What are they doing here, do you know?"

"Lumber camp. They make good timber men. First class cruisers and flume men, I hear. Flint doesn't use them — he's from the northern end of the state and is suspicious of everything from below the Line. They all work for Brush Vane's outfit, the Cibola Timber Company."

CHAPTER XI

Hatfield left the battered private car in a thoughtful frame of mind.

"I can't see Brush Vane being back of an attempt on my life," Jaggers Dunn had declared in the course of their subsequent conversation. "He's ruthless, arrogant, domineering, yes. But that's the result of many years during which he had been a law unto himself, undisputed leader of a faction that has dominated this end of the state. Yes, I've had business differences with him from the first. He refused us a right-of-way across his land and we were forced to invoke the Act of Eminent Domain before we could build. He was set against railroads — just as set as the element you spoke of, the lawless element that hangs out in the Espantosa Hills. Then when he found he could not stop construction, he immediately set out trying to maneuver things to his own advantage.

"He tried to corner the beef market and make a deal with me which would eliminate all competition and abrogate solely to himself the privilege of supplying our camps with meat. I turned that down cold, for I feel that the small ranchers should share in all benefits that accrue from the coming of the road. He put over a deal with Cosgrove of the L & W — they're thick as thieves — and froze out certain small ranchers, including that poor devil, Hudgins, who was murdered last night in the course of a saloon brawl, I hear."

"Vane and Flint don't get along over well, I understand," Hatfield remarked.

"No. Flint outsmarted him in a timber

deal a couple of years back, before this section had any inkling of railroad building here. We kept the secret pretty close until we were ready to commence operations. Flint and Cosgrove of the L & W don't get along any too well, either. I understand they had a row over cross-tie prices, but Flint still sells to the L & W. Vane can't supply all their demands for lumber, or I suppose he would have hogged that also, and Cosgrove is forced to buy from Flint as well as from Vane. Not that Vane has any kick coming there, however. The two roads just about take the entire available supply of lumber the section affords.

"And now with the building boom in the offing in town, Vane and Flint will be hard put to supply the demand. I imagine they'll bring in new equipment shortly and expand operations. Vane is making a good thing from the coming of the roads, despite his resentment and animosity. Most of which, I feel, is just damn contrariness. No, I can't see him instigating a deliberate attempt on my life."

But Hatfield, recalling a man's life, choking in the grip of Brush Vane's great hands, was not so sure.

What he did not tell Dunn, for reasons of his own, was that he shrewdly suspected that the attempted dynamiting was not directed at the railroad builder, but at himself. "I downed three of those half-breed hellions since I lit in this section," he mused. "They aren't going to let that pass."

The concentration furrow between his black brows deepened.

"But blowin' a feller up with dynamite isn't any Yaqui or 'Patchy trick," he muttered. "There's somebody with a lot more white blood than any of that bunch has got that's doing the thinking for them. What I've got to find out for sure is — who!"

Swiftly he ran over the events of the preceding day. Several occurrences, recalled to mind, caused his brows to draw even closer together. He pondered the fight in the restaurant and the attempt at knifing young Sheldon Vane.

"And the jigger Vane was slugging it out with was Austin Flint's lumber camp foreman, I learned," he mused. "Yes, looks like those two outfits are going to get together sooner or later."

He reached the open space upon which the railroad station fronted. It was black with men, all gazing in the same direction. Hatfield paused on a little elevation near the outskirts of the crowd and listened to the gabble of comment.

"Ol' pay-car oughter round de curve most any time now," said a voice whose liquid consonants could come only from a shiny-toothed mouth set in a shiny black face. "Boy, I done been waitin' fo' dis minute fo' thirty days and seben million pick swings. Ol' pick stood in corner today, though. Boy, I'se all set to step wide and han'some!"

"I aims to be first in line today," said another voice belonging to a giant track layer with bowed shoulders and a deeply lined face.

"First paid off, first busted," remarked a companion. "Me, I ain't in no hurry. Figure on sendin' most of my pay back east to the Old Lady, anyhow."

"That's doin' the right thing, brother," said another. "Wish I had somebody to send *my* pay to. Them gals over to the Sluicegates'll get most of mine before come dark. And what'll *I* get — a headache!"

"I craves likker, cards, wimmen and action!" bawled a little feller about knee high to a duck. "C'mon, pay wagon! Ain't seen nothin' but holes in my pockets for a month now."

Suddenly one of the straining outposts down the track let go with an excited yelp. Peering in the direction indicated by a score of pointing fingers, Hatfield saw a tiny black

112

dot swing around the distant curve where the rails, shimmering in the heat, drew together and were lost in the vastness of the desert. Swiftly the dot grew, a whitish plume trailing away behind it, until it resolved to a panting engine drawing a single coach. As the sunlight glinted on shiny windows and glittering gold paint, the crowd cheered wildly and began to form in a long line with much wrangling and jostling for place.

Up to the station boomed the pay car, rattling over switch points, swerving suddenly as a ready yard man threw a switch and shunted it onto a spur which paralleled the open space beside the station. The engine purred and hissed, grimy enginemen dropped down the steps and headed for the restaurant. A hostler climbed into the cab, tested the water, banked the fire and settled himself comfortably on the engineer's seat.

The pay car door flew open with a cheerful clatter, two heavy-jowled railroad policemen took up their stations on either side of the grated window and the first worker, the giant track layer, swung up the steps to receive his little trickle from that golden flood that was to pour into Espantosa.

Before the barred door would clang shut again, more than three thousand men would share in the bright coins that spun swiftly from the paymaster's hands. And before another dawn, the vast majority of those yellow counters would roll across the green cloth of the gambling tables, clink musically on the "mahogany" of the Sluicegates and the other saloons, drop into the ready hands of the dance-hall girls.

Another dawn and the roaring, swaggering army would be "busted," headachy, bleary-eyed and cotton-mouthed, but grinning with pleasant memories as the clattering construction trains boomed westward again and the bitter battle with desert and hill and mountain gorge began anew. Thirty days of sweat-stained toil, of hardship and danger, then another riotous twenty-four hours of delirious pleasure.

From his perch on the little mound, Hatfield watched the long queue shuffling toward the pay-car. His green eyes were sunny with a sympathetic light and his rather wide mouth quirked at the corners. The Lone Wolf could understand and appreciate these simple, gregarious toilers, although he could never be one with them. And he saw in them a symbol of the new era that was coming to this land of huge distances, untold wealth and unlimited opportunity.

Behind him sounded a sudden clatter of

racing hoofs, a chorus of shouts, a musical jingle of bridle irons. He turned and saw, racing up the crooked main street, the hilarious, untrammelled, life-lusty signs of the era that was drawing to a close — the era of the open range, the unfenced ranch, the vast uncounted herds. Whooping shrilly, with tossing manes, and ringing hoofs, the Slash K cowboys careened around a bend and out of sight, their uproar dying to a drone in the distance.

Riding hard on their heels, came a compact group of sober-faced punchers, considerably fewer in number. These, Hatfield deduced, were the Lazy H boys riding to town after burying their boss, Cal Hudgins. He wondered what they thought of the new owner, Doris Carver, and how the little redhead would make out. Ranch hands, as a general thing, did not take kindly to a woman owner. They resented petticoat rule, and such a spread often experienced difficulty obtaining and holding good riders.

He wondered what would be Brush Vane's attitude toward the girl, the niece of the man whose death, it was openly said, he had instigated. Then there was the complication of Vane's son, young Sheldon. That the boy was more than casually interested in Doris Carver, Hatfield felt confident. And that he was fiercely loyal to his father was plainly evinced by the way he had taken Austin Flint's camp foreman down a peg the night before.

"Oh, there's merry hell aplenty ready to boil," the Ranger growled as he headed uptown.

Already the construction town was beginning to boil. The bars were crowded. So were the gambling hells, the dance-halls. There was a shriller note to the turmoil. The gabble of voices was attaining a higher pitch. The jostling throng in the street was growing hilarious. Song was bellowing from open windows, and profanity, and rabid argument. An angry yelling was going on somewhere, punctuated by a woman's wrathful screech.

Old Sheriff Rider strode past, mumbling under his moustache. He gave Hatfield a glance of scant friendliness and nodded shortly. Behind him sauntered his lanky chief deputy, Blaine Collier. Collier had a lean, brown face that did not move a muscle, and a gray eye that twinkled. His nod to Hatfield was much more cordial than the sheriff's.

A moment later, Hatfield saw Brush Vane. He was standing in front of the Sluicegates Saloon, talking with a heavy-bodied, corpu-

116

lent man whose sharp-nosed face seemed ludicrously small as compared to the rest of him. Hatfield wondered who the man could be. His clothes were not of rangeland cut and the hand with which he rubbed the sharp bridge of his nose was white and plump and soft of palm.

Hatfield entered the saloon and shoved his way to the bar. The loquacious bartender of the night before was on duty. He greeted Hatfield as an old acquaintance and hastened to pour him a drink.

"Saw your old bunky, Brush Vane, standing outside as I came in," he remarked with a jerk of his thumb toward the swinging door.

Hatfield nodded. "Who's the feller with him?" he asked casually.

"The fat feller? That's the big boss of the L & W railroad — Bije Cosgrove."

"The L & W president?"

"Uh-huh. He's a city feller, but ain't a bad sort. Spends free, and they say he runs that railroad right up to the hilt. Giving old man Dunn a tough fight of it, I hear tell. Lots of folks are betting he beats Dunn to the Southwest and gets them big contracts for his road. Me, I'm hopin' for to see Dunn win out. Cosgrove's nose is too darn sharp to be to my liking."

Hatfield was about to reply, when a sudden yelling across the room drowned his voice. Almost instantly the yelling was followed by a roar of gunfire.

Chapter XII

Jim Hatfield whirled toward the outer door of the saloon. Blue smoke was wisping up and there was a mad swirl of men trying to get out of range of flying lead. Hatfield was engulfed in the panic-stricken crowd as he tried to force his way across the room.

Another shot sounded, then a thud of swift feet. The saloon doors swung wildly and the Ranger had a fleeting glimpse of two men hurriedly leaving the room. He shoved men aside, became entangled in a screeching group of fleeing dance-hall girls and it seemed to him that minutes passed before he won free and reached the neighborhood of the door.

Two men lay on the floor. One was clutching a shoulder with crimsoned fingers and alternating groans and curses. The other, a grizzled, lanky individual, lay very still, a rapidly spreading red smudge staining the front of his gray flannel shirt. His unfired gun half protruded from its holster. Another gun lay beside the wounded man.

Facing across the bodies of the wounded men were two tense groups, one considerably outnumbering the other. A glance told Hatfield that they were Slash K and Lazy H cowboys. Hands were gripping guns, eyes were gleaming with hate. A single untoward gesture or word would send those guns flaming into action.

Unhesitatingly, the Ranger strode between the hostile groups. His slim, bronzed hands were close to the black butts of the heavy Colts flaring out from his lean hips, his eyes were icily cold. His tall figure and bleak face seemed to dominate the situation. Before he spoke a word, hands dropped from gun butts, tense muscles relaxed.

"That'll be enough," he said in the quiet voice of assured authority. "This feller here is hard hit and needs attention."

"And he's going to get it, too," blared a squat, powerful individual, sawed-off shotgun in hand, both barrels at full cock, who had ranged himself beside Hatfield. It was Runt McCarthy, head bartender and part owner of the Sluicegates. Behind him were two of his drink jugglers, likewise armed with shotguns. And McCarthy was known as a peace-loving man who promoted order with buckshot.

"What the hell's this all about?" demanded

119

McCarthy.

"Them two new Slash K hellions," bawled a Lazy H puncher. "The tall one drilled poor Tom Gibson dead center. Tom never had a chance: his gun didn't even clear leather."

"Gibson reached first," declared a Slash K rider. "Monty had to shoot in self defense."

A wild gabble of voices, rising higher and higher, followed. Hatfield's cool tones cut through the turmoil like a silver knife through clabber.

"Let this feller with the punctured shoulder talk," he said, looking up from where he knelt beside the grizzled man. "How'd this thing start, feller?"

"I don't know," groaned the wounded man. "That tall black-faced jigger said somethin' to Gibson. Gibson said somethin' back and reached for his gun. The tall feller downed him. I was going for my hogleg when the little feller with him let me have it. Them two hellions is fast, too damn fast."

Hatfield nodded, baring the breast of the grizzled man and exposing a blue hole just above the left breast. He noted the free flow of blood with relief. That meant less danger of serious internal hemorrhage. But the wound was a bad one. Gibson breathed

120

hoarsely and his face was ghastly.

"Bandages," the Ranger snapped over his shoulder, "and somebody call a doctor if there's one in this damn town."

"They done gone for Doc Thorne," shouted a voice.

A bartender shoved a roll into Hatfield's hand and the Ranger proceeded to deftly bandage the wound. He eased Gibson to the floor and turned his attention to the other wounded man. He had a hole through his shoulder, high up. No bones were broken and the Ranger knew he'd be good as new within a month. He asked no more questions, being convinced that the truth of the affair could only be had from the principals. Gibson was unconscious, and the man who shot him was among those missing.

Sheriff Nat Rider came bustling through the swinging doors, his lank deputy sauntering at his heels. Rider gave Hatfield an accusing glare.

"Seems you're always around where there's trouble," he growled.

"And it appears, Sheriff, you're always some place else when it busts," Hatfield replied calmly.

Somebody laughed. Sheriff Rider's white moustache bristled from a scarlet face and he sputtered in his throat. Blaine Collier, the deputy, rubbed his "hound-dawg" chops with a bony hand and regarded Hatfield thoughtfully. His expression was that of a man who is struggling with elusive memory. However, he said nothing, and appeared mildly amused at the sheriff's angry sputters.

The doctor, an old frontier practitioner, arrived at the moment. He examined Hatfield's bandaging and nodded approval.

"Go on and get drunk," he told the shoulder-drilled cowboy. "I've seen fellers scratch themselves worse than that. We'll take Gibson to the railroad hospital. He'll pull through, I figure, but he'll be laid up for a couple of months. The Lazy H is sure havin' a run of tough luck — first the owner and then the foreman of the spread."

They carried Gibson out, the Lazy H punchers, with menacing eyes and compressed lips, clumping behind the stretcher. Sheriff Rider went looking for the two gunmen. The Slash K riders drifted to the bar and the gambling tables. Hatfield went back to his neglected drink.

"I saw that feller that shot Gibson," the barkeep told him. "Mean lookin' feller, tall and thin, black as a Mexican, but didn't look like one. Eyes like gimlets. The other was a little rat of a jigger that couldn't keep his hands still. Wonder where Brush Vane got them?"

Hatfield wondered, too. A little later he left the Sluicegates and began a systematic round of the various bars, gambling houses, and dance-halls.

The autumn afternoon wore on. The brass blue sky turned to gold. Gold, too, was the mist of dancing dust-motes churned up by the countless feet pounding the unpaved street. And still that golden flood poured from where the pay-car stood in the railroad yards. It takes time to pay off three thousand men in gold and silver coin.

The roar of Espantosa took on a deeper note, interspersed with hysterical highlights of sound. Roulette wheels spun faster. Dancing feet thumped and clicked a wilder rhythm. Bartenders ceased pulling corks. They deftly knocked off the necks of bottles and sloshed the whiskey into glasses held by impatient hands. Splinters of glass didn't matter. It was easier on the stomach than Espantosa whiskey, anyway.

The air of the saloons was blue with tobacco smoke. At times it was blue with smoke of a different kind — the acrid, grayish smoke of burned gunpowder. Sheriff Rider swore in more deputies, and swore himself black in the face. Steel flashed in a dark hand. The sawdust, already sodden with spilled whiskey, was splashed crimson. Three minutes later the man who had been cut was drinking with his still dripping forearm around the shoulders of the man who had knifed him. Both had already forgotten what the row was about.

Still the steady stream of gold poured into the town, and still it poured across the whiskey-soaked bars, across the green cloth of the gambling tables, into the clutching hands of the women.

But there is a limit to human rapacity just as there is a limit to human endurance. The bartenders began to slow up, and, as the lookouts and proprietors became increasingly bleary-eyed, surreptitious fingers slipped coins into ready pockets.

The pale gamblers in their somber black relieved only by the immaculate white of their shirt fronts, began to grow ruddier of visage as numerous slugs of straight whiskey took effect. Their coldly calculating play became less calculating and some of the gold stream reversed itself across the green cloth.

Girls who had been carefully hoarding the gold lavished on them by generous admirers began buying drinks of their own accord. Soon the hands that had clutched avidly at coins "earlier in the morning" were throwing them onto the bars with wild abandon. Rounds of drinks on the house became more frequent.

All of which added to the sweet serenity of Espantosa. Where the construction town had roared, it now howled and screeched. The crash of breaking glass and splintering furniture added to the pandemonium. Yells, shrieks, raucous laughter and weird cater-wauling rose in a swirling miasma of sound to the shuddering stars.

And to the north the cathedral arches of the pines, splashed with moonlight, ebon with shadows, towered in somber peace, the music-haunted peace of Nature's own minister. Here the eternal solitude and the wind-needled silence seemed to voice dignified disapproval of the petty strivings, the misguided passions and the falsely guided ambitions of the human ants swarming under the reddish "stars" of the construction town. It was a compassionate disapproval, that of the stately trees, the moonlight and the velvet shadows, the uncensoring understanding of the mighty Mother of all growing things striving, ofttimes by devious and mistaken paths, toward the light.

But the "disapproval" of the grim hills to

the southwest seemed somehow subtly different. Espantosa Canyon, like a grinning mouth of snaggy teeth set in festering jawbones, leered toward the settlement and the gaunt crags fanging up against the moon-drenched sky hung over the shack town like poised spears ready for the cast. Perhaps that was the howl of a wolf upon some lonely star-burned ledge. But then again it may have been the wail of a passing soul ripped from its quivering clay in Espantosa's hell-dives under the lurid light of smoking lamps, amid the reek of spilled whiskey and sweat and smoking blood. And that whimpering wail *might* have been an owl in the tree tops, or it might have been the echo of a dying man's scream bubbling in his blood-filled throat; or the tear-choked sob of a woman's disillusionment and despair.

And the stern old hills undoubtedly resented this unwonted invasion of their silence, their solitude and their age-old privacy, and added on their ledger a woeful debit that must some day, and soon, be paid in terror and in pain.

Or so it seemed to Jim Hatfield as he paused at the outskirts of the railroad yards and gazed westward toward the shouldering hills, austere and forbidding, against the silver spangle of the stars. It was with a tightening at the back of his throat that he turned again to the quest he had been pursuing for hours.

And then, unexpectedly, in a sordid saloon that seemed little affected by the gayety farther uptown where the lights were brighter and the streets more crowded, he came upon his quarry, the mysterious Monty, the man who had shot Tom Gibson.

Chapter XIII

A window of the saloon opened onto the shadowy street, and through that window he had a clear view of the interior. Straight across the squalid room he gazed to where, directly beneath a window in the far wall, two men sat at a table.

One of the men was beefy, broad of beam, with a sharp-nosed face too small for the rest of him. Hatfield instantly recognized him as Bijah Cosgrove, president of the L & W railroad. He was engaged in earnest conversation with his table companion.

The second man was tall and spare, clad in black with only the white of his shirt front to relieve his somber garb. He was exceedingly swarthy; dark almost as an Indian. But Hatfield noted that his cast of countenance

127

was not that of a red man. The cheekbones were too low, the nose, though prominent, was not aquiline, neither was it fleshily broad, as is often a characteristic of the Apache or the Lip. There might possibly be a dash of other blood, but the man was predominantly white.

"Spanish, maybe," the Lone Wolf muttered, standing back from the light streaming through the window, "hair looks it."

The man's hair was lank and intensely black with a peculiar "dead" look to it.

This was Monty, Brush Vane's "new hand" who had shot Tom Gibson, the Lazy H foreman, he felt sure, recalling the bartender's description of the man.

The man's dress puzzled him for a moment. The Lazy H punchers had spoken of Vane's "new hand" and Hatfield had immediately associated the term with cowboy, a rider almost invariably being indicated when the term hand was employed. Monty's garb was certainly not that of a "rannie," but the Ranger recalled that Brush Vane's activities were not limited to ranching. The man spoken of as Monty might well be employed in some other capacity, one having to do with Vane's lumber enterprise, for instance.

For a moment Hatfield stood in the shadows, uncertain as to his next move. He was curious as to what was the subject of conversation between the L & W president of doubtful antecedents and this lean, swarthy individual who had "professional gunman" written all over him. But he felt sure that if he entered the saloon, the conversation would cease or the subject be quickly changed.

Nobody here, other than Jaggers Dunn, knew him for a Ranger, he was confident, but since landing in the section, he had been mixed up in too many incidents to pass unnoticed; and men did not hold confidential conversations in the presence of strangers about whose motives they might well be dubious.

With another glance, Hatfield moved on down the street. Abruptly he halted. He was on the lip of the steep bank below which lay the railroad yards. Directly beneath him he could make out the roofs of a string of freight cars on a siding. On a parallel track, stood the pay-car, now dark and deserted and locked up for the night. Its engine had been uncoupled and ran ahead a car length or so to facilitate fire cleaning. Dumped ashes still smoldered between the rails. The engine, with fires banked, purred contentedly with occasionally idling air pumps and a feather of steam drifting lazily from its safety valve.

All this Hatfield saw at a glance. He also saw that the saloon sat on the very edge of the bank, its foundation shored up by timbers that projected over the lip. Where he stood, the shadows were deep. He measured the distance to the boxcar directly beneath him, glanced over his shoulder once, and then leaped lightly to the top of the car, a couple of yards below.

He landed on the balls of his feet with a barely audible thud. The car rocked a little on its springs with a creaking sound; otherwise there was silence. Apparently no one in the yards or on the street had noticed the leap.

Hatfield glided to the end of the car, leaped across the opening and ran along the catwalk to a second car. Now he was in the deep shadow cast by the squat saloon building. He could barely make out the projecting end of one of the shoring timbers. Reaching up, he gripped the beam with both hands and swung his long body up until he was astraddle of it.

He got to his feet, teetering on the precarious perch and clinging to the side of the building for support. Balancing carefully, he leaped again and reached the edge of the bank in safety. Now he was behind the saloon. A narrow alley ran between it and a huddle of shacks.

There were shacks all along the lip of the bank, he noted. No lights were visible. The occupants were apparently either asleep or attending the pay day festivities up town.

A bar of light, cutting the shadows with feathery gold, marked the window beside which Cosgrove and the man Monty sat. Hatfield glided toward it, planting his feet with the utmost care, silent as the shadows themselves, which might conceal anything, or nothing. Once he thought he heard the tiniest of sounds somewhere near, like the shifting of a body's weight upon a numb foot, but his straining eyes could see nothing in the darkness, and the sound was not repeated. After a moment's rigid pause, he moved on until he was crouched beside the window.

Through the opening drifted the hum of the room, an unintelligible jumble of words and various drinking sounds. Then voices became audible and at the sound, Hatfield's long body stiffened and the concentration furrow deepened between his black brows.

"You figure on staying placed where you are, despite that trouble tonight?" remarked one, a high treble, the kind of a voice often

131

possessed by a fat man.

" 'Low to," said a second voice, deep of tone. "That trouble don't mean anythin'. Dozen men ready to swear I shot in self-defense, after Gibson had reached."

"Is Gibson going to die?"

" 'Feard not, judgin' from what I heard. He would have, I callate, but that big hellion that's been makin' trouble ever since he showed up took care of him before he got to bleedin' good."

The voice suddenly vibrated with anger and underwent a subtle change of quality.

"Who is that feller, anyhow?" it demanded. "And where did he come from? And what's he doin' here?"

"I spoke to Vane about him," said the whining treble. "Vane is of the opinion he's some tough gunfighter the — the *opposition* has brought here. He went to visit Dunn today, you'll recall. And incidentally, *that* job was bungled badly."

"Everything consarnin' that hellion's been bungled," growled the other voice. "The next one won't be."

"Vane said he never saw a man draw a gun so swiftly," said the treble voice, with apparent irrelevance.

The other voice dripped with deadly menace.

"There's lots of things Vane ain't never seen before — and there's something that tall jigger ain't never seen before, either."

The other seemed to understand the implication. "I know your reputation, Monty, but don't be too confident and take unnecessary chances. You're playing a dangerous game."

"The stakes are high enough to be worth it."

"Quite right. You're still acquiring stock?"

"So much we sure don't want to get caught short."

"With both Hudgins and Gibson out of the way we won't be. The girl should be easy to handle, under the circumstances."

"Maybe, but we got to work fast or somebody might get ahead of us. I know somebody that'd like to get hold of that spread. He —"

Behind him, Hatfield heard the faintest of sounds. It was but the hiss of a deeply drawn breath, but it sent the Lone Wolf away from the window in a plunging leap. Steel slashed downward in a vicious stroke, the knife glinting a silver arc in the light streaming through the window. A curse of rage followed the stroke.

Before the knife could fling up for another blow, Hatfield was upon the wielder, a slight wiry man whose muscles seemed to be of tempered steel. He writhed from the Lone Wolf's grip with unbelievable strength, threw up his long blade and lunged with it as with a sword, the whole weight of his body behind the reaching point.

Hatfield ducked, diving low, and the steel that was meant for his throat whizzed harmlessly over his shoulder. He gripped the small man by the thighs, whirled him into the air and hurled him over his shoulder.

Straight through the open window spun the body, arms and legs revolving wildly. It struck the table with a prodigious crash, overturning it, sprawling the fat man, Cosgrove, on the floor amid the wreckage of his splintered chair.

Hatfield had a glimpse of blazing, narrowed eyes in a swarthy face. He hurled himself to the ground as a gun roared, gushing lances of reddish flame through the window. He wriggled sideways as the slugs whined over his head, jerked his own gun and flung it up.

Inside the saloon boomed another shot, then a crashing jangle. Hatfield fired at a vague figure inside the suddenly dusky room. A crackling report echoed the blast of his own gun, another jangle and crash. Darkness like a black blanket enveloped the interior of the saloon, through which howled curses. There was a terrific banging and thumping, a jingle of breaking glass, a slamming of doors.

Hatfield leaped to his feet, smoking gun in hand, staring at the black window square.

"Hellion shot the lights out and hightailed," he growled. "Or maybe he's still inside there, waitin'."

Tensely he stared at the window square, watching for the slightest move. The racket inside was lessening as men spun through the swinging doors as fast as they could reach them.

Suddenly the texture of the black square subtly changed. It was still opaque, but the opaqueness was now acrawl with a reddish overtone. There was a dull boom and with appalling abruptness a wall of yellow flame gushed up inside the room. One of the shattered oil lamps had exploded.

Hatfield leaped back from the light that blared through the window. For an instant he hesitated, then he turned and ran fleetly up the alley. He passed the corner of the saloon, raced by half a dozen shacks and finally skirted one to reach the street. Holstering his gun, he walked rapidly but unhurriedly toward the crowd that was shouting and milling in front of the blazing saloon. With keen eyes he scrutinized faces, but nowhere could he locate either Cosgrove, the lean gunman, Monty, or the wiry little man who was doubtless Monty's companion and who had evidently been posted to keep watch on the saloon while Cosgrove and Monty held their conference.

"Hope I busted the little sidewinder's neck," the Lone Wolf growled. "Fanging out of the dark that way. If he hadn't drawn that deep breath when he flung his arm up, he'd have let daylight through me for sure. It was him I heard in the first place and he was creeping up behind me all the time."

The saloon was blazing merrily and already the fire had communicated to the nearest shacks. Hatfield eyed the conflagration with concern.

"The whole damn town's likely to go," he muttered, "not that there would be much lost. Just save 'em from tearing it all down when they start building permanent."

There was open space between the huddle of shacks that fringed the yards and the town proper, however; and with little or no wind blowing, he doubted if the flames would leap the space. A sudden yell brought a more serious development to his attention.

"Look at the way the fire's dropping over

onto them boxcars," bawled a voice. "They're burning already."

A gabble of excited comment followed. Then a terrified screech —

"There's a dozen cars of blastin' powder in that string! When that lets go it'll blow this whole section clean to Mexico!"

For an instant there was numbed silence, then a frenzied stampede away from the yards. Men pounded up the crooked street, howling and whooping. Hatfield, jostled, butted, all but knocked from his feet, found himself alone in front of the burning building.

Chapter XIV

His mind racing swiftly as his feet, Hatfield sped to the lip of the bank and glanced down. Flaming planks and charred ends of beams were raining upon the roofs of the boxcars. The tinder-dry wood was burning briskly in a score of places. The Ranger stared at the fiery tongues whipping in the faint breezes. Now he recalled seeing that string of cars when, earlier in the day, he had paused beside the pay-car. He remembered the ominous red placards adorning their sides. The powder cars, destined for the construction work farther west, had been placed here on this siding to be as far as possible from the yard activities and stray engine sparks. There was not a switch engine anywhere in the vicinity, even allowing that the crew would take a chance on snaking the explosives out of the siding before the fire got to the powder.

"And if it lets go there, it'll do just what that jigger said," Hatfield muttered. "It'll blow this town and the yard and everything in it clean to Mexico."

For a crawling instant of indecision he hesitated. Should he run back to town shouting a warning? Hell, no! What would be the use? The drink-befuddled revelers wouldn't even understand what was going to happen until it happened and the majority of them woke up in some hot place with coal shovels in their hands. And then there were the railroad men in the yards and the shops and roundhouse. They wouldn't find out what was in store for them until too late. And it was but a matter of minutes until the flames ate their way to the powder.

Even as the thoughts raced through his mind, Hatfield was going into action. A plan was evolving in his brain, an utterly reckless plan promising but a possibility of success.

Once again he leaped over the lip of the bank and landed upon the roof of the car immediately underneath. It was the third from the upper end of the string. Hand over hand he dropped down the ladder to the ground and raced to the switch stand. He threw the switch, opening the siding to the main yard lead. Then he ran to the switch which opened the pay-car siding onto the lead. This he threw in turn and ran up the siding to where the purring engine stood with fires banked and a full head of steam in its boiler. He made sure that the rear coupler was open and the knuckle set at the proper angle for an automatic coupling. Then he whisked into the cab and gripped the throttle, thanking the good Lord for the vacation months he had once spent on a fireman's seat-box. He released the engine brake, cracked the throttle. There was a complaining cough from the stack, a hiss of steam, and the great drivers slowly turned. The stack boomed wetly and there was an ominous thudding in the cylinders. Hatfield kicked the lever that opened the cylinder cocks. Steam gushed out on either side, and jets of water that had condensed in the cylinders. The stack boomed again, the drivers turned and the locomotive moved down the siding and clattered onto the lead.

Hatfield slammed the throttle shut, put on the brake and dropped to the ground.

He ran back and closed the switch, raced to the cab, after making sure the knuckle of the coupler was open and threw the reverse lever over. He eased the engine back against the burning powder cars. He heard the couplings clang together, threw over the lever and widened the throttle. The big drivers spun with a roar of clashing steel on steel. Hatfield muttered an oath, twirled the sand valves and sent streams of sand gushing under the drivers. The ponderous tires gripped the sanded rails, held. The couplers clanged and the powder cars began moving toward the lead.

Hatfield glanced back. The roofs of half the cars were blazing fiercely now as the breeze set up by their motion fanned the flames. Very quickly the roofs would burn through and start dropping blazing embers onto the powder containers. After that it would be touch-and-go. The containers wouldn't take long to get hot enough to set off the powder. And Hatfield hated to think how many tons of explosive were thundering along behind him.

Down the long lead boomed the great engine, her siderods clanking a wild song, steam and smoke spouting from her stubby stack. Hatfield caught a flickering glimpse of men running, waving their arms and yelling. Everybody in the yard seemed imbued with a desire to be elsewhere. Hatfield didn't blame them.

Less than a hundred yards ahead glowed a red light, low down. It was the marker at the switch from the lead to the main line — a switch that would be locked.

Hatfield estimated the distance, waited until the last second before he slammed the throttle shut and applied the brakes. The drivers slid on the rails, the couplers banged and jangled. For a crawling instant Hatfield feared he had miscalculated and that they would hit the derail that protected the switch, and derail the engine. He was out of the cab before the wheels stopped revolving. The pilot was almost over the switch points when the flaming train ground to a stop.

Hatfield jerked one of his guns and fired at the lock. The second slug knocked it to splintered fragments of metal. He threw the switch and raced back to the engine. The Ranger and his cargo of death and destruction roared onto the main line.

A glance at the steam gauge told him the pressure was dropping. The water showed low in the glass. He jerked open the inspirator and sent a stream of water gushing into the straining boiler. He leaped to the deck, flung the fire door open and bailed in coal, scattering it expertly to get the best and quickest results. The steam gauge needle was rushing when he swung onto the seat-box. He glanced back at the blazing cars, glanced ahead along the track. Everything was clear. The yard lights were dropping behind. A little farther and the explosion would damage nothing but the cars and the engine — and the Ranger, if he still happened to be around.

The engine careened around a curve. Hat-field started to close the throttle. But directly ahead, its towering super-structure spidering against the sky, was a long bridge that spanned a dry wash that in time of rains was a roaring torrent. Before Hatfield could do anything about it, the flaming train was rumbling across the bridge.

Hatfield swore an explosive oath. If he stalled the train on the bridge, the explosion would blow the structure to kingdom come. And with it would blow any chance the C & P had of winning its race against the L & W. Still swearing, he widened the throttle.

The length of the bridge seemed intermi-nable, and before he was half across it, a new horror intruded into the picture. Hat-field was not very familiar with the railroad schedule, but he did know that the night passenger train was due in Espantosa somewhere around this time. And he had to get at least a thousand yards from the bridge before it would be safe from the explosion. His mind worked at racing speed. He dived across the cab, flung open the fireman's seat-box. He muttered relief as he saw the greasy, spiked cylinders of red fuses inside. He grabbed one, kicked open the little front door beside the boiler and went clutching and teetering along the narrow catwalk that led to the front end of the engine. Bracing himself against the hand rail, he tore the protecting cap from the fusee and scratched the two ignition surfaces together.

The fusee sputtered, caught fire. Hatfield swung down to the front sill of the engine and drove the spike firmly into the wood. He reeled and staggered back along the catwalk and dived into the cab. A glance at the steam gauge showed him the pressure was still okay. He swung onto the engineer's seat-box and proceeded to get the last atom of speed from the already racing locomotive. A backward glance showed the fire eating down the sides of the box cars.

The train roared off the bridge and thundered down the main line. Hatfield estimated the distance they covered — five hundred yards — seven hundred — nine — a thousand! He slammed the throttle shut and braked frantically.

The death train ground to a stop once more. Hatfield dropped to the ground, ran back and jerked the coupler open. He propped a stone under the raised pin to assure it would not drop again, and tore back to the cab. He opened the throttle. The coupler jangled as the knuckle opened. The engine raced ahead, gathering speed with every turn of the wheels. The red glare of the burning fusee flickered on trees and crags. The fiercely blazing cars dropped behind.

And around a curve less than a thousand yards distant blazed the headlight of the night passenger.

Chapter XV

Hatfield saw the plume of steam-streaked smoke rising from the engine's stack cut off and billow out as her engineer closed his throttle. Streams of sparks shot out on either side as the brakes took hold. Then the stack roared again, shooting up clouds of smoke streaked with clots of fire. The engineer had his locomotive working in reverse.

Hatfield also had his throttle closed and was doing everything he could with the brake. He threw the reverse bar over and jerked the throttle wide open. The great drivers spun in reverse, planing off long shavings of steel from the screeching rails. But with scarcely slackened speed, the two howling locomotives rushed toward each other. Hatfield braced himself for the crash that was sure to come.

The world seemed to explode in jagged flame as the two locomotives came together. Hatfield was hurled forward. His head struck the boiler with stunning force and for an instant, blackness engulfed him. The bellow of escaping steam pouring from smashed joints aroused him. Dimly he could hear voices yelling through the uproar.

Then all else was drowned by a thunder that shook the eternal hills themselves. The stars paled to a yellow glare. Displaced air screamed past. The derailed engine rocked and swayed. Hatfield felt blood well up in his nostrils; a deadly nausea gripped him and for a long moment he lay stunned, his senses reeling, his limbs floundering aimlessly.

Finally he clawed his way to his feet, his ears still deafened, his eyes blinded by the concussion and glare of the fearful explosion. He reeled through the steam-filled cab, slid down the steps to the ground and staggered away from the shattered locomotives.

Passengers — screaming, bruised, terrified — were pouring from the coaches. Trainmen ran about, waving lanterns and yelling. The passenger engineer, swabbing blood from his face with his sleeve, stumbled forward to meet Hatfield.

"Feller," he said thickly, "when I first saw you bearing down on us, I figured you were plumb loco or hootched up. Then when that blast let go, I decided you were the Devil moving a load of Hell. What in blazes is this all about?"

Hatfield, his brain clearing, his legs beginning to behave, told him as much as he thought advisable. The engineer wagged his bloody head and stared his admiration.

"Feller," he said, "if I hadn't lost my hat, I'd sure take it off to you. Guess you saved that infernal town from going to hell sooner than expected. A little bit ago I was cussing because a derail in the Crater yards held us up and we were twenty minutes late. Reckon now I'd better be thanking the good Lord it happened."

"If it hadn't happened, the chances are that about now you'd be trying to explain to Him about things you've done in the past," Hatfield replied. "Like as not we would have met on the bridge which would have been interesting."

"Damn interesting," growled the hogger. "And if you hadn't snaked that powder out of town, we might have hit the yards just about the time it let go."

He turned to the passengers who were crowding around, volleying questions. "Folks," he said, "when and if you say your prayers tonight, put in a word for this big jigger and remember if it wasn't for him, mighty likely you wouldn't have had the chance to say 'em."

The voice of the conductor interrupted. "Here they come!" he shouted.

Glancing back toward the distant bridge, Hatfield saw the sparkle of a headlight, far up the track.

"That'll be the wreck train, coming to pick up the pieces," said the engineer. What they'll need is a couple of hundred steam shovels to fill in that hole up there. Looks like a short section of the Grand Canyon! Guess old man Dunn must still be in town. Nobody else could have got 'em rolling that fast."

The wreck train screeched to a stop, its headlight glaring across the scene of de-

struction. Lanterns bobbed about as trainmen and officials skirted the wide crater
hollowed out by the explosion. Foremost
was General Manager Dunn, who evinced
little surprise when he sighted the Ranger.

"Had a notion it was you snaked those
cars out of the yard," he remarked as he
shook Hatfield's hand. "You're always
smack in the middle when hell busts loose."

He took Hatfield by the arm and led him
aside.

"How the devil did that fire start?" he
asked.

Hatfield told him, in terse sentences,
Dunn nodding his head from time to time.

"I ordered a light engine to follow the
wrecker," he said when Hatfield finished.
"Come on, we'll head back to town and
make arrangements to have this mess
cleaned up. We can talk on the way."

"What I'd like to know," Hatfield said as
they skirted the crater, "is how is Cogrove,
the L & W president, tied up with a character like Monty, who's a habitual gunslinger
if I ever saw one."

"That's your question," grunted Dunn.
"You're the Ranger. I'm just a railroader."

Hatfield nodded. "Get the answer, and we
may get the answer to quite a few things,"
he commented. "Now here's something

else, something that may be of significance to you. I'll repeat what I heard, word for word, as near as I recall that particular fragment of their conversation. Cosgrove asked, 'You're still acquiring stock?' Monty answered, 'So much, we sure don't want to get caught short.' Then Cosgrove said, 'With both Hudgins and Gibson out of the way, we won't be.' There was more to it — I'll tell you the rest later — but that one is a puzzler. In the range country, stock is synonymous with cattle, but I'll bet my last peso Cosgrove and Monty aren't buying cows. Just what kind of stock would they be likely to acquire?"

"I'd say the answer is obvious," Dunn replied. "Railroad stock."

"C & P stock?"

"Not likely. Our stock is on the market, of course, but it is an investment stock, not the kind speculators are interested in. C & P quotations don't fluctuate."

"Suppose you win out in this race to the Southwest, would that cause C & P quotations to shoot up?"

Dunn shook his head. "Would make for very little change," he declared. "Certainly not enough to warrant somebody buying up large blocks for speculation purposes. This new line is just incidental to the C & P system, as you very well know."

This time Hatfield nodded. "And how about L & W stock?" he asked.

"That would be a horse of another color," Dunn admitted. "Their quotations would shoot up to beat the devil. But that angle doesn't make sense. The race is a neck-and-neck affair at this moment. In fact, despite the obstructions placed in our way, I'd say we have the edge. Something the L & W bunch know as well as we do."

"Then if Monty is buying up all the stock he can get hold of, it looks like they've got an ace up their sleeve, something you don't know anything about, right?"

The empire-builder swore, and looked decidedly worried.

"Looks that way," he admitted, "but what the devil could it be? They darn near had it played for 'em tonight. Right now they'd have gained considerable, if it hadn't been for you. You saved a score or more lives by getting that powder in the clear, and the devil only knows how much in property damage. But they couldn't have counted on that, seeing as it was an unpredictable accident that fired the cars. What's the answer, Jim?"

"I don't know," Hatfield admitted, "but I've got a hunch that it was something to do with Cal Hudgins' ranch, judging from the way they congratulated each other over having got both Hudgins and Gibson out of the way. They 'lowed the girl would be easy to handle, whatever they meant by that."

Dunn swore helplessly, and glanced up the track to see if the engine that would bear them back to town was in sight.

"One of two reasons, I'd say," Hatfield replied. "He may have had some reason for wanting to shut Gibson's mouth. Gibson may know something they want kept quiet. What they said sort of hints at that. But there's another angle to consider."

"What's that?"

"Some naturalists maintain that a large parasite in its stomach is what drives a weasel to its unbridled ferocity and wanton killing. I think the chronic gunfighter is perhaps a human parallel. I sometimes think there's a maggot gnawing in his brain, that urges him on to killings. Their psychology is a peculiar one and seems to develop strength as they go along. They'll go hunting for some jigger with a reputation as a quick-draw man, just to prove they're faster and more accurate than he is. It's a strange urge. Some sheriffs are called hanging sheriffs. They are at their happiest when they're looping a rope around somebody's neck. Just another manifestation of the blood urge. As I said, Monty has all the earmarks of the professional killer, and Gibson is a pretty hard looking specimen, too. That's what may have been back of that shooting. Just one gunfighter looking for trouble with another one. It's darn important for us to find out for sure. If Gibson doesn't die, he may do some talking. What I'd like to know more than anything else is, just who and what is Monty. Seems he works for Brush Vane, in some capacity. He's not a cowhand, although he may once have been one. He's not punching cows for Vane, that's sure."

"Shouldn't be hard to learn in what capacity he works for Vane," observed Dunn.

Hatfield nodded. "I'll take care of that," he said, "but to get back to that stock business. You should be able to find out who is buying L & W stock in unusual quantities."

"Yes," Dunn agreed. "Doubtless the deal would be handled by a broker. I'll pull a few wires and find out who the firm is and who they're buying for. Somebody may be working under cover, but you can't hide sales, and there are usually ways to get information. I'll get to work on it right away. Well, here comes that damned engine. Let's go back to town. I've got things to look after, and I imagine you could do with a little rest. You've had a busy day. Incidentally, the local folks who invested in the C & P project owe you a vote of thanks. If that stuff had let go in the yards or on the bridge, it would have just about knocked us out of the race."

When they reached town, they discovered, as Hatfield anticipated, the saloon had been destroyed by the fire that, however, had been quickly brought under control and had done no further appreciable damage. The hullabaloo had but little affected the pay day hilarity, which was still going full swing.

Tired though he was, Hatfield did not immediately go to bed. Instead, he repaired to the Sluicegates Saloon. Escaping from a crowd of pawing, vociferous admirers, he engaged a bartender in conversation.

"Nope, the sheriff didn't find Monty and that other hellion," the barkeep replied to a casual question. "Reckon Monty went back to the lumber camp. Rider wouldn't go out there tonight. He's got other things to keep him busy."

"Monty works for the lumber company, then," Hatfield commented.

"Uh-huh, that's right," said the drink juggler. "He's Brush Vane's timber cruiser.

Spends most of his time prowling around through the woods, spotting trees ready for cutting. Don't show up in town for a week sometimes. Understand he's mighty good at the work. Vane sets a heap of store by him."

Hatfield nodded his understanding. A timber cruiser's profession is an exacting one, requiring extensive knowledge of timber growth coupled with instinctive natural ability. On a cruiser's estimates may rest the difference between profit and loss of an undertaking.

Shortly afterward, Hatfield went to bed, but not to sleep for quite a while. The recent events had him decidedly puzzled. His thoughts dwelt on the saturnine Monty who, it appeared, kept weaving in and out of the jumbled picture like a black cat through moonfire.

"And where did I hear that hellion's voice before?" he asked himself in exasperation. "Somewhere recently, I'm willing to bet. Something he said reminded me all of a sudden of something I'd heard somebody else say. Can't remember that, either. Things got too mixed up right afterward and the word or sentence, whichever it was, that impressed me slipped clean out of my mind.

"And another thing. If Monty is buying up L & W stock, who is he buying it for?

Not for himself, unless he's something totally different from what he pretends to be. And not for Cosgrove, I'd say. In fact, I'd say that Monty is running things, not Cosgrove. He appears to have Cosgrove under his thumb. And that's another poser. How, and why? And Monty works for Brush Vane. Looks like *Senor* is mixed up in most everything going on hereabouts."

One angle relative to Vane was fairly clear: his motivation, if he were really working with such men as Cosgrove and Monty. Vane didn't need money, but he worshipped power and would be loath to relinquish the supremacy in the section he had enjoyed for so long. As a prime moving force with the dominant railroad faction, his seat in the saddle would be doubly secure. But would Vane countenance the things that had been going on of late? Hatfield knew sometimes a man finds himself the captive of developments. Vane might have gradually, unthinkingly gotten in so deep it became impossible to pull out. That could be the answer.

"Oh, the devil with it!" Hatfield growled to himself. "I'm going to sleep."

Which he proceeded to do.

He was awakened the following morning by someone pounding on the door.

"Couple of fellers downstairs to see you,"

said the voice of Hamhock Harley. "Mighty anxious to have a powwow with you, and seein' it's 'most noon time, I figured you'd be about ready to get up."

Upon descending the stairs, Hatfield found the two elderly rancher friends of the dead Cal Hudgins — Mack Bush and Sam Gerard.

"Son," remarked the former, favoring Hatfield with a quizzical glance, "son, do you always raise hell and shove a chunk under a corner like you been doin' ever since you hit these diggin's?"

Hatfield grinned down at the oldster and his green eyes were sunny.

"Well, not always," he admitted. "The last couple of days is sort of unusual, I figure."

Gerard knit his grizzled brows and his gaze was speculative.

"You sort of remind me of somebody I've heard tell of," he said. "I can't exactly place who right by the minute."

"I've been mistaken for lots of folks," Hatfield smiled in reply.

Old Sam snorted derisively. "That sounds mighty likely," he grunted with elaborate sarcasm. "When they made you, feller, they busted the mold."

"Which brings us down to business," Bush put in. "Things is sure busted up over to the Lazy H, what with poor ol' Cal bein' done in and then Tom Gibson gettin' laid up with lead pizen for a spell. What we was in a mind to say was that the little lady over there is sort of up against a tough trail. With both Cal and Tom Gibson out of the running, the Lazy H boys hardly know whether they're coming or going. They ain't a bad bunch, with rope or brandin' iron, but they ain't none of 'em particular heavy above the eyes. They can do what somebody tells 'em to do, and do it pretty well, but that's about all. Sure ain't nobody in that bunch of mavericks that's capable of runnin' a spread as it ought to be run, particular a spread that's been havin' trouble like the Lazy H has of late."

"Which sort of brings us down to the nubbin'," put in Gerard. "Son, did you say you was aimin' on stayin' put in this section for a spell?"

"Well," Hatfield replied, "anyway, I'm aimin' to stay for as long as I'm here."

The oldsters digested this gravely. "Appears reasonable," admitted Bush. "Admittin' such, it's also reasonable you can use a job?"

Hatfield nodded, divining what was coming. "Appears reasonable."

"And the Lazy H can sure use a foreman

with some get-up-and-go to him," Gerard declared emphatically. "We gabbed it over with the little lady and she agrees you're the feller for the job, if you'll take it."

Hatfield thought swiftly. He had deduced from the conversation between Bije Cosgrove and Monty that Cosgrove was desirous of obtaining the Lazy H ranch.

Hatfield wondered why. So far as he had been able to learn, there was nothing exceptional about the spread, which was small, a goodly portion of it consisting of a section of the bleak Espantosa Hills, surrounding Espantosa Canyon of unsavory reputation.

But men like Cosgrove do not often act without a definite motive. If Cosgrove wanted the Lazy H, he had some urgent reason for warning it. Cal Hudgins had been murdered out of the dark, and the shooting of Tom Gibson smacked of premeditated murder. Monty might well have goaded Gibson into reaching for his gun, knowing that the Lazy H foreman wouldn't stand a chance. Monty could then plead self defense and get away with it.

"I'll give it a whirl," he accepted tersely. "Just how do you get to the spread?"

He rode out of town in the early afternoon — westward toward the glowering Espantosa Hills, where Espantosa Canyon gaped like the grinning jaws of a skull. Eyes watched him go. And in the shadow of the hills, death waited.

Chapter XVI

The Lazy H ranch house sat in a grove of cottonwoods less than half a dozen miles from the mouth of Espantosa Canyon. Hatfield decided that the spread was not a bad one for a hill range, and he liked the looks of the trim little ranch house with its old-fashioned porches and tiny inner court. Barns, corrals and outbuildings were in good repair and arranged with care and judgment.

The Ranger did not pause at the bunkhouse, but rode straight to the front veranda of the ranch house. He dismounted, left Goldy tied to the evening breeze and knocked at the door. There was a shuffling of slippered feet in the hallway and a moment later an ancient Mexican woman stuck a wizened countenance through a narrow opening of the door.

Hatfield bared his black head and bowed with grave courtesy.

The Mexican woman regarded him from twinkling beady eyes that registered approval.

"Come," she said, and turned and shuffled along the hall.

He followed her and a moment later was ushered into the main living room of the ranch.

Hatfield was more than a little surprised, but didn't show it.

Seated at a table was Doris Carver, the late afternoon sunlight casting glints of ruddy gold from her coppery hair. And seated opposite her was Austin Flint.

It was Flint who showed surprise, a surprise evinced in a tightening of his already tight mouth and a slight narrowing of his deep-set, tawny eyes. With the light behind him his eyes looked almost black.

Doris came to her feet with a rush and her greeting was frankly cordial.

"So Uncle Sam and Uncle Mack actually persuaded you to come!" she exclaimed. "I was afraid they wouldn't be able to. You arrived at a good moment, too, for I need advice. Do you know Mr. Flint?"

Hatfield nodded to Flint, who returned the greeting.

"Mr. Flint just brought me a proposition," explained Doris. "He wants to buy the Lazy H and is offering me a very fair price. Would you advise me to sell? You know what I've been up against since arriving here."

Hatfield hesitated. Flint was then the "other person" Cosgrove feared might obtain the Lazy H spread. He recalled also Jaggers Dunn's remark that Flint and Cosgrove had had business differences.

While he hesitated, Flint spoke.

"I just bought the R Bar 7 to the southeast of this range," he said in his deep voice. "I 'low the two of 'em would make a pretty nice spread. I vowed I'd never go in for cattle again when I left the Panhandle, but you know how it is — pullin' away from the range ain't so easy as you figure."

"Yes, it gets you, once you've known it," the girl put in soberly. There was longing in her voice, and that as much as something which he was still unable to define decided Hatfield.

"It's been my experience, Ma'am," he said mildly, "that when somebody wants to buy something from you, it's likely to be worth as much to you as it is to him."

The girl's eyes brightened. "That's just the way I feel about it," she declared, "and now that you are here to help me straighten things out, I'm sure I can make a go of it. No, I don't think I care to sell at present, Mr. Flint, but thank you for the offer just the same."

For a moment Austin Flint hesitated, and

there was a glitter in his eyes. But he rose to his feet and smiled, a smile that did not get beyond his lips.

"Sorry, Ma'am," he said affably. "Mebbe you'll change your mind some time, and if you do, my offer stands."

With a nod to Hatfield, he took his departure. Doris Carver watched him go with thoughtful eyes.

"That's the second offer I've had in the past twenty-four hours."

"Yes?"

"Yes. An offer came from Mr. Brush Vane." Her eyes flashed resentment.

"As if I would sell to my uncle's murderer!"

"You don't know that Brush Vane had anything to do with your uncle's death," Hatfield reminded her. "Who brought you the proposition?"

The girl's eyes softened and there was a faint touch of color in her cheeks when she replied:

"His son — Sheldon Vane."

For the next few days, Hatfield rode the Lazy H range, familiarizing himself with the spread. His initial opinion was quickly verified and he wondered why Brush Vane and Austin Flint, to say nothing of the L & W president, Cosgrove, were so anxious to obtain the little ranch. A living could be made on the range, but that was about all. Was there some secret in the hills, he wondered, that gave to it a value not otherwise apparent. Mineral deposits, for instance. Metal is sometimes found in unexpected places.

With this in mind, he examined the hills and gorges with an engineer's eye. He rode the rim of Espantosa Canyon for a couple of miles, but the geological and petrological formations were identical with the rest of the terrain, so he decided to by-pass the brush-choked, boulder-strewn gorge, for the time being.

He summed up his conclusions in a terse paragraph.

"Well," he told Goldy, "you might as well expect to find metal in a grindstone as in these rocks. Not a piece of quartz anywhere. No signs of oil or coal, or even of base metals that might be worth working."

There was considerable timber on the hills, but Hatfield quickly decided that because of the ruggedness and inaccessibility of the terrain, the cost of working it would doubtless be prohibitive, especially when the large holdings of Vane and Flint were taken into consideration.

"Nothing that I can see except fairly good hill cow country," was his final decision. "Now why in blazes do a bunch of jiggers want to get hold of the spread? I'm beginning to believe everybody in this section is loco, and if things keep going as they have of late, I'll be all set to join up with the rest of the brainless terrapins. Already started talking to myself, and that's a bad sign."

To the east, he noted, the hills merged with the real timber belt beyond the Lazy H holdings. He asked a question or two relative to the cuttings.

"If you follow that ridge up there, you'll come onto Brush Vane's big camp and the head of his flumes," a Lazy H puncher told him.

Hatfield followed the ridge the next day. Again he rode the cathedral aisles of the pines, with the purple shadows thronging about him and the wind-music of myriad needles sighing over his head. The woodland covered the flanks and shoulders of the ridge with a dense growth and only along the spiny crest was there a scarcity of the towering conifers.

Once, from the bare head of a beetling crag, he had a glimpse of Espantosa, a straggly town of children's building blocks huddled in the lap of the hills, with the desert stretching away in a golden infinity toward the pale green of the rangeland. Far, far to the east, the Nueces was a silver thread banded with emerald.

The forest became more profound as he rode eastward, the spires of the pines more towering, their shaggy buttes more gigantic. Less frequently was the deep blue of the shadows splashed with liquid amber or molten bronze. Here the sun could but rarely pierce the olivine interlacing of the needles. The bright winged sunbeams died far far above in the depths of the glaucous pools formed where the extremities of the branches strove mightily toward the sky.

Some time after passing the site of Espantosa, Hatfield heard, thin and clear, the bright-edged voice of ringing steel.

There was something clean and refreshing about the cheery sound of gleaming ax blade biting through tough wood fibres. Later the monotonous whine of a saw added its undertone. Then he heard the rushing purr that was the water of the flumes. Along that liquid road the huge logs hurtled down the mountainside to plunge sullenly into the pools below, where brawny jacks with peavies would "ride herd on 'em" and guide them to where cable and gripper would snake them to the chattering mills or to the hoists that would swing their ponderous lengths to waiting flat cars.

The growth thinned out as Hatfield rode on. Soon he reached an open space a-bustle with activity. Here the logs from the cuttings were assembled at the flume heads. The jingle of chain traces, the snorts of horses and the shouts of men mingled in a cheery pandemonium.

Hatfield rode on until he was beside one of the flumes. Sitting his golden horse, he gazed at the stream of swift water in a wide wooden trough.

It was deep, that rushing stream, for often the great logs were more than six feet in diameter at the base and the water had to be of a depth sufficient to prevent them knocking the bottom out or splintering the sides of the flume.

For some distance the flume ran at a gentle grade. Then it dipped over the lip of the ridge and from there on hurtled giddily downward.

Further on were other flumes, into which the shaggy brown buttes were being dumped; but the one beside which he paused was free of timber at the moment.

Turning in his saddle, the Ranger glanced up a higher slope that backed the ridge at this point. It was clear of timber for nearly a

166

quarter of a mile. Then the fringe of growth cut darkly across the sun drenched expanse.

As he gazed, a man rode out of the timber belt. He was mounted on a superb black horse and closed the distance swiftly. As he approached, Hatfield saw that it was Brush Vane.

Recognition was mutual. The giant's grizzled brows drew together and he eyed the Ranger with scant friendliness. Hatfield sat unmoved under the truculent glare. Vane rode on without halt or deviation and pulled up between the Ranger and the flume, and only a yard or so distant. His voice rang out harshly —

"This is private property, feller."

"Well," drawled the Lone Wolf, "I'm not taking any of it away with me."

Vane seemed nonplussed for a moment at the unexpectedness of the reply. Then his craggy countenance flushed.

"I ain't looking for no smart talk from you," he rumbled.

"You started the talking," Hatfield reminded him quietly.

Vane's face took on an even darker flush. He spurred his horse toward the Ranger, a ham-like fist swinging against his thigh.

Whether Vane intended launching a blow at him, Hatfield never knew. For as he swayed back easily in his saddle against that possibility, there was a whistling crack that split the air before his face. A chill breath fanned his cheek.

Before the whiplash crack of the distant rifle reached his ears, Hatfield heard Brush Vane give a queer, gasping grunt. Blood streaming down his face, the timber baron pitched sideways from his saddle. Hatfield lunged to seize his arm, but Vane's great weight, down-surging, tore the arm from his insecure grip. With a sullen plunge the giant's body vanished in the swirling waters of the flume.

Chapter XVII

For a tense instant Hatfield was numbed to inaction by the unexpectedness of the tragedy. Then, as Vane's flaccid body broke surface and began to move swiftly down the flume, his voice rang out —

"Trail, Goldy!"

Instantly the great sorrel leaped forward, racing parallel to the flume. In a single lithe movement, Hatfield shucked off his heavy double cartridge belts with their sagging guns and flipped them around the saddle horn. Then he swung his right leg over the horse's back and stood poised in his left stirrup.

Vane was either killed or knocked unconscious by the slug from the unseen rifle. If only wounded, he would be drowned before reaching the pool at the far end of the flume. There might be yet time to pluck his swiftly-moving form from the water before the flume dipped over the lip and mill-raced down the slope.

Gauging the distance with care and nicety, Hatfield poised on his unstable perch. Goldy, straining every muscle, swiftly closed the distance between the floating body of Brush Vane. A scant score of feet from the lip, he overhauled it. Tensing his muscles and holding his balance by a miracle of agility, Hatfield leaped. He struck the water almost alongside the body of the timber baron. He clutched wildly and gripped Vane's collar. And then they were over the lip and rushing downward on the breast of a roaring flood.

Gasping, sputtering, half-drowned and wholly deafened, Hatfield fought to keep the wounded man from being dashed against the timbered sides of the flume or forced beneath the surface. He managed to keep Vane's face above water, but he himself was submerged repeatedly.

Once he swerved slightly and red flashes stormed before his eyes as his head grazed the timbers. But the felt of his wide hat held firmly in place by the thong tied under his chin, and his thick hair, saved him from being knocked unconscious.

Again, his foot struck and he was conscious of a numbing pain in his ankle. Gasping and choking, he wriggled over on his face, gripped Vane's huge body the tighter, and fought to control the progress of his unwieldy burden.

In a kaleidoscope of greens and browns, the timber growth blurred past. Through the spray, Hatfield had a glimpse of a sheet of water, far below, its sullen green dotted with the shaggy lengths of huge logs. Should they strike one of those massive timbers, they would be but bloody pulp sinking swiftly to the bottom of the pool. He set his teeth as the pool rushed toward them with frightful speed.

Vane was recovering consciousness. His feeble, misdirected movements added to the Ranger's problem. Unless he was able to keep them both head on with the rushing stream, they were lost. He gripped the giant with iron fingers, hauled his head around, held him rigid.

The pool was before them! They were over

it! A great timber loomed beneath, its shaggy bark like the coat of some carnivorous beast. Hatfield could make out every fold and tracery as they shot over it, grazed its rounded side and struck the water with a mighty splash. He was dimly conscious of wildly shouting voices as, the breath knocked from him, his lungs filled with water. He fought feebly to rise from the turgid depths, dragging the thrashing form of the timber baron with him.

Men were boiling through the shallows, plunging into the deep water, gripping him with strong hands. An instant later he was stretched on the bank of the pool, breathing in great gasps, coughing the water from his lungs.

Brush Vane was the first to recover for the bullet had only creased his scalp. He levered himself on a shaking elbow and stared, almost in awe, at the gasping Ranger. He raised a hand and traced the shallow furrow just above the left temple. Then he stared again at Hatfield.

After a final fit of coughing, Hatfield sat up. He grinned, rather feebly, at Brush Vane. The latter solemnly extended a huge hand.

"Feller," he said, his deep voice shaking with emotion, "if there's ever anything in this world, no matter what, I can do for you, just say the word."

The lumberjacks clustered around the pair set up a cheer. Hatfield chuckled as he got to his feet, a little shakily. He shivered in the cool autumn breeze.

"Well, first thing," he grinned, "you can have some of these jiggers hunt up a couple of good rough towels and then show us a warm place where we can use 'em."

They were being hurried to a nearby engine house when a clatter of hoofs sounded on the slope above.

First came Goldy, bridle jingling, his black mane floating in the breeze. His saddle was empty save for Hatfield's gun belts swinging from the horn. Behind him a man was forking Brush Vane's tall black horse, kicking his glossy ribs with spurless heels. He yelled congratulations as his eyes fell on the two dripping figures.

Hatfield held out his hand and the sorrel thrust a velvety muzzle into the hollow of it, nickering softly the while.

"I couldn't keep up with that hellion, no matter how hard I tried," said the man on the black.

"Goldy goes where I go, whenever he can," Hatfield smiled.

"Here comes Mr. Monty," exclaimed the lumberman on the black. "He was ridin' the timber edge when it happened and headed this way likkerty-split."

The tall, black-haired man rode swiftly to the group and his dark countenance mirrored concern.

"You all right, suh?" he asked Vane. "I saw it all. The hellion that plugged you must have been over just a mite to the right of where I was ridin'. I got a dozen of the boys scoutin' the timber for him. When they get him, I callate there'll be a hangin'."

"You hang that kind *after* you get 'em," Vane grunted. He turned to the Ranger.

"This is my boss, timber cruiser and estimator, Al Monty," he introduced.

Hatfield supplied his name and Monty extended a hand dark as an Indian's. The Ranger's gaze lingered for an instant on the supple fingers, then raised to Monty's swarthy face.

"Howdy," he nodded, "how's things over west?"

Monty's eyes glinted in the shadow of his low drawn hat brim, but his face was devoid of expression or recognition as he replied.

"Can't say, Hatfield, I ain't been in that section for quite a spell. I'm from the timber country up by the Oklahoma line."

"I was just judgin' from your riding rig," Hatfield explained.

"I bought it down here," Monty replied. "Can't 'low as I particular care for this deep saddle."

After they had rubbed up a vigorous circulation with the towels and somewhat dried their clothes by the warmth of the engine room boiler, Brush Vane turned to Hatfield.

"Come along over to my ranch house, for chuck," he invited. "Ain't but about an hour's ride by way of a short cut through the timber I use."

The sun was low in the sky and the ride back to the Lazy H a long one. Hatfield decided to accept the invitation. A little later, he found himself riding through the lower pine forest, along a trail that he recognized as the one on which he had so nearly lost his life the day he arrived in the section.

That he was right was soon proved when a broken, fire-eaten stump with one white splinter standing ten feet or so in the air appeared alongside the trail. On the far side of the trail was a welter of top and branches. The huge trunk had been sawed away and removed.

Vane noticed his glance and jerked his thumb toward the stump.

"Lucky nobody was ridin' this way when

that feller come down," he said. "Fell plumb across the trail just a few days back. I ride this trail nearly every night. Came nigh to busting my neck when I rode into that top in the dark."

Hatfield turned in the saddle. His gaze rested on the timber baron's face.

"You ride this way quite frequently, then?" he asked.

"Uh-huh, quite often," Vane replied. "It's a shortcut from the camp to my house. The trail across the north pasture is easier riding, but it's nearly four miles longer. I usually ride this way when I get stuck late at the camp and am in a hurry to get home."

"Anybody else ride this trail regularly?"

"Nope," Vane said. "Hardly anybody ever rides it, especially at night."

Hatfield hesitated, then asked still another question.

"The night Cal Hudgins was killed, did you ride this way that night?"

Vane shot him a swift suspicious glance, but replied without hesitation.

"Nope," he said. "I'd intended to, but changed my mind at the last minute. Remembered my range boss mentioning a water-hole on the north pasture that he figured should be blown out and dredged. Decided to take a look at it."

Hatfield nodded, and was silent; but as he gazed at the dark "caves" between the great tree trunks, and the tangle of undergrowth, he experienced an unpleasant tingling along his spine. During the rest of the ride through the woodland, his eyes were constantly probing the surrounding terrain.

"Hope Monty managed to run down that dry-gulchin' hellion," Vane growled.

"Monty looks like he's good at gettin' things he goes after," Hatfield commented.

"Uh-huh," agreed Vane, "best timber cruiser and estimator I ever saw. Dropped down this way a month or so back and applied for a job. After I'd talked with him awhile I put him on, and it sure wasn't no mistake. I figure to have plenty for him to do before long. I'm figuring on addin' to my timber holdings. Lots of good trees farther north.

"Monty can estimate a stand quicker and more accurate than any man I ever met. Funny jigger — rides off into the woods and is gone for two, three days, but always comes back with valuable information."

"He's the feller that had trouble with Tom Gibson of the Lazy H a few nights back, isn't he?" Hatfield asked.

Vane's face darkened. "Uh-huh. Most everybody of my outfit is having trouble with somebody or other of late. Ever since that hellion Austin Flint showed up here. He beat me out of a valuable stand of timber and then turned a lot of folks against me."

"Flint paid the price you asked, didn't he?" Hatfield asked.

Vane turned a truculent glare on him. "Sure, but I didn't figure it to be worth so much then. That was before the railroads come along."

Hatfield grinned and his green eyes were sunny on the timber baron's face.

"Then the thing Flint really did that he shouldn't was get the best of Brush Vane in a deal?"

For an instant Vane seemed on the verge of an explosion. Then unexpectedly his craggy features split in a grin. His throaty cackle was almost pleasant.

"Feller," he said, "you have a way of puttin' things that ain't easy to answer."

As the growth began to thin, Hatfield again suddenly turned in his saddle and let the full force of his long green eyes rest on the timber baron's face.

"Mr. Vane," he said, "a little while back you told me if I ever wanted a favor from you, not to hesitate to ask."

"That's right," Vane agreed heartily, "and

I meant it."

"Well," said Hatfield, "I'm going to ask one right now."

"Shoot!" said Vane. "I set considerable store by my life, and right now I guess that belongs to you. Ask anything you want, and it's yours, half of my holdings if you want 'em."

"Wouldn't know what to do with them if I had them," Hatfield replied, with a smile. "What I'm going to ask you is not to ride this trail again, especially not at night."

It was Vane's turn to twist in his saddle. He stared at the Ranger.

"What the devil?" he sputtered. "But never mind. Guess it ain't much to do for a feller who's just saved your life — ride a few extra miles, which is all it amounts to. But would you mind telling me why you ask?"

"You just said," Hatfield smiled, "that your life belongs to me. Well, if that's so, I'd sort of like to keep it up and kicking for a while."

"Now what in hell do you mean?" demanded the bewildered rancher.

"Just this," Hatfield replied, "I've a feeling if you keep on riding this dark and homely trail at night, the time's coming when it'll be your last ride. Remember that tree lying

178

across the trail? Mr. Vane, that tree did not fall by accident. It fell the night I rode into this section, and came within an inch of killing me. Only my horse's agility saved me. And that was the night you did *not* ride this trail, although you planned to do so, as doubtless quite a number of people knew. That tree was arranged to fall when somebody rode under it, and that somebody, according to somebody's way of thinking, should have been you."

In a few terse sentences he explained the ingenious and devilish contraption by which the fall of the tree had been governed.

Brush Vane swore until his horse snorted and shied. "I'd never have believed folks hate me so damn much," he concluded bitterly.

Hatfield smiled a little. "Mr. Vane," be said, "how long have you lived in this section?"

"All my life," Vane replied.

"And have known the folks hereabouts all your life. Right now can you call to mind a single man of your acquaintance who would be capable of trying to kill you in such a manner?"

"No," Vane admitted, "I can't. There are fellers who would walk up to me and gunshoot me, if they thought they could get away with it and not get plugged first, but I don't know anybody hereabouts I'm scared to turn my back on."

"Exactly," Hatfield nodded.

"But what the devil — who does want to do me in?" demanded the bewildered rancher.

"That," Hatfield admitted frankly, "is what I don't know, and what I would very much like to know. But somebody sure planned carefully to do for you."

"And of all the goddamned snake-blooded ways to do it!" snorted Vane.

"Yes, it was devilish, and smart," Hatfield conceded. "You would have been found dead under a fallen tree. The kind of accident not at all uncommon in timber country. Nobody would have thought much of it. They'd have buried you and forgot all about it. Just a plumb accident, that's all."

Vane swore some more, and rubbed his bullet-creased head.

"One thing is certain," Hatfield summed up, "somebody sure wants to get you out of the way."

"I've got enemies," Vane grunted.

"Yes," Hatfield agreed, "but we've just about decided that none of them would employ such methods."

"Well, I'm damned if I know who it could

be then," said Vane. "Of course, he began hesitantly, "there's that infernal railroad, but, damn it! — although I ain't got no use for Dunn, I can't see him going in for such a thing. He's uppity as hell, and a fighter, but I'm ready to bet my last peso he's a square-shooter. It hurts me to have him think I might have something to do with what's been happening to his railroad. I don't work that way, Hatfield."

The Ranger nodded. He had just about arrived at the same conclusion.

"I can't see why anybody should want to do it," Vane continued. "You got any idea?"

"I'd say," Hatfield replied slowly, "that it is because you know something."

Vane looked blank. "What?" he asked.

Hatfield smiled wryly. "If I had the answer to that, or if you were able to tell me, things would be different hereabouts," he replied.

Vane swore some more. Suddenly he again twisted in his saddle and stared at the Ranger.

"Hatfield," he said slowly, "just who are you?"

"You know my name, and it's my real one," Hatfield replied. "Right now I'm range boss for the Lazy H."

"So I gather," Vane remarked dryly. He stared at Hatfield a moment longer, but evidently decided to refrain from asking questions he felt would not be answered.

Soon afterward they rode from beneath the somber arches of the pines, crossed a belt of rangeland and pulled up at the big white ranch house of the Slash K.

Young Sheldon Vane was on the veranda when they rode up and he greeted Hatfield with marked cordiality. He was silent during the evening meal, however, and later departed, a morose expression shadowing his normally pleasant face. Brush Vane stared after him with worried eyes.

"Can't figure what's the matter with the boy of late," he said. "Don't seem to take no interest in nothin'. Just passed his twenty-first birthday, too, and I've always promised him he could start out on his own then. I heard tell the Lazy H spread was for sale and I told him I'd buy it for him. Appears, though, that niece of Hudgins didn't aim to sell. Maybe that's what's botherin' Sheldon."

Hatfield had other opinions as to young Sheldon's trouble.

Refusing an invitation to remain for the night, he rode to Espantosa. He had spent the evening studying Brush Vane and had arrived at no definite conclusion. Vane had his good qualities, Hatfield felt confident.

But he was arrogant, stubborn, and high-handed. For too many years he had been the ruling power in the section. It would take a few more jolts to shake his complacency and his belief in his own views.

Vane had a good opinion of Bije Cosgrove, because Cosgrove, apparently at least, accepted his opinions. He had scant use for Jaggers Dunn because Dunn had opinions of his own, many of which clashed with his own. Also, he had developed a sense of injury toward his neighbors.

"The hull kit-and-passel of the district figures I had Cal Hudgins done in," he rumbled in the course of the evening's conversation. "I never did nobody in that weren't standin' up to me man to man. I don't have to have my killin's done for me by somebody else, out of the dark. I leave that kind of stuff for dry-gulching hellions like the one that took a whack at me this afternoon."

Hatfield wondered whether the bullet that creased Vane's head had been meant for the old cattle baron or for himself. It might easily have been directed at either one. He recalled that he had swayed back in his saddle the instant before, in anticipation of the blow Vane looked like he might strike. The sudden and unexpected move could have been enough to spoil the dry-gulcher's aim.

And the too-pat appearance of Al Monty on the scene was not without its significance. Also, he had other things to think about — things that went a long way to substantiate a startling theory he was evolving about Al Monty.

"Just fingernails," he mused as he rode to town. "A fingernail is a mighty little thing to hang a man by, but you never can tell."

When he shook hands with Al Monty, Hatfield had noticed that despite the Indian darkness of his hands, *the cuticle of his fingernails showed a line of pink!*

In Espantosa he contacted Jaggers Dunn.

"Well," said the G.M., "I've gotten the lowdown on that stock deal, and it's a queer one. Somebody has been hammering down L & W stock. Industriously spreading rumors that the C & P is bound to win the race to the southwest. L & W quotations have dropped accordingly. And somebody, a gent who goes by the name of Albert Stone, has been buying up all the loose blocks. Dealing through a New York brokerage firm."

"Albert Stone," Hatfield repeated thoughtfully. "Did you learn anything about him?"

"Not a darn thing," Dunn confessed.

184

"The transactions are conducted by mail, from San Antonio. Only address used by Stone is a postoffice box. He sends payments in cash — registered mail. Funny way to do business."

"Darn funny," Hatfield agreed.

"But eccentrics have been known to do that before," Dunn added. "And the brokerage firm doesn't give a damn so long as they get paid. They never bothered to look up Stone. Why should they?"

Hatfield nodded. "And like as not the man who registers the letters is not Stone," he said. "By the way, though, the L & W runs through San Antonio, doesn't it?"

"That's right," replied Dunn. "And so do other railroads, including the C & P. Why?"

"Nothing, except that it wouldn't be much of a chore to get to San Antonio from here, and back again," Hatfield answered. "And wouldn't take too much time, either. Something to remember."

"I don't know what the hell you're driving at, but I'll remember it," said Dunn.

"I'll talk to you about that later," Hatfield nodded. "How's the work coming along?"

"Everything's going along so smoothly, I'm worried," Dunn growled. "Nothing out of the way has happened for several days. We're forging ahead by the hour."

"Sounds good," Hatfield commented.

"Uh-huh," Dunn grunted, "but my experience has been that when things get to going too good all of a sudden after you've been up against hell for a long time, look out for trouble. I'm looking, but damn it! I don't know where to look. Have you learned anything, Jim?"

"Nothing definite," Hatfield confessed. "I'm getting a hazy notion as to who is back of all the hell-raising, but so far it's just a notion. Nothing much concrete to base it on. But for the life of me, I still can't see any reason for a lot of funny things. Just don't make sense. I'm still convinced that darn Lazy H spread is somehow the key to the mystery. And that *sure* doesn't make sense. Why the devil does everybody in the section all of a sudden want to buy that mess of hills and rocks?"

"I don't know," Dunn replied gloomily. "If you can't figure it out, don't expect me to."

After a little more futile discussion, Hatfield went to bed. He headed back to the Lazy H shortly before noon the following day.

His route led across a particularly vicious strip of desert. Clumps of weird buttes, chimney rocks and pinnacles rose unexpect-

186

edly from the sands. There was nothing of vegetation other than Chola cactuses brandishing crooked arms. And aside from a deadly sidewinder or two in the shadow of a rock there was nothing of animal life.

Hatfield was approaching a forbidding cluster of buttes of great extent, known as The Devil's Kitchen, when he perceived not far from the trail the figure of a man crawling painfully on hands and knees. He seemed to be striving to reach the shade of the chimney rocks. The sun beat down upon his head, which was unprotected save for matted black hair, and he appeared to be in the last stages of exhaustion.

"Poor devil must be hurt," the Ranger muttered, quickening Goldy's pace.

Near the base of the nearest butte, the crawling man collapsed, his face buried in the hot sand, his limbs moving feebly. Hatfield turned Goldy from the trail and a moment later swung down beside the prone form.

At the sound of the horse's hoofs, the man strove to raise his head, but let it fall again, lolling on the sand. From his gasping mouth sounded a hoarse croak.

"*Agua!* Water! *Madre de Dios! Agua!*"

Hatfield freed his canteen from where it hung. Kneeling he removed the stopper and lifted the scrawny form in his arms. The thin, dark face stirred an elusive chord of memory as the black eyes blazed with an exultant light. He strove to fling erect as movement flickered from behind the butte, but the man wound arms like bands of steel about him. Before he could burst the grip asunder, a gun barrel crashed against the back of his skull. With a muffled groan, the Lone Wolf fell forward on his face. The man he had befriended leaped to his feet with a curse and viciously kicked the prostrate form.

CHAPTER XVIII

Hatfield came back to consciousness with the sound of voices in his ears. He was prone on his back, the hot sun beating on his upturned face. His head ached intolerably and when he strove to ease its position, he found that he could not. A band passed across his forehead, holding his head rigidly in place. He gradually realized that there was another band across his throat, still others across his body. He was spread-eagled on the sand, his wrists and ankles secured to stakes driven into the ground.

All this he sensed vaguely as he lay struggling with a deadly nausea. Instinct rather than reason caused him to refrain from opening his eyes or struggling. Nothing was in the range of vision of his slitted lids, but as his mind cleared, he could make out what was said by the unseen speakers.

"Hadn't I better take his guns?" demanded a querulous voice.

"No," said another and deeper voice. "Folks recollect the kind of guns a feller carries. Somebody might spot 'em. Don't touch nothin' he's got. Fork yore bronc and let's get goin'."

"Maybe we'd better run down that damn yellow horse and do for him," suggested the querulous voice. "I don't know how I missed pluggin' the sulphur colored hellion. I swear to God he dodged the bullet."

"That horse is trained," said the second voice, "and he's been shot at before. He's back in the rocks somewhere out of sight, and he'll keep out of sight. Even if somebody does come along and spots the horse, the Devil's brandin' irons will have done for that jigger by then. Come on, let's get goin'."

A moment later Hatfield heard the thud of departing hoofs, growing fainter as the seconds passed. Cautiously he opened his eyes and tried to stare about.

His range of vision was extremely limited,

but what his glance first fell upon caused him to stare in bewilderment.

He lay beside the spire of the chimney rocks. The rock was cracked and serrated, and in the cracks, short lengths of wood had been driven, evidently with a definite plan in mind. There were three of them, set at different heights and stepped back along the wall, the one nearest him being the lowest. And from each length suspended by thongs, were two glass bottles filled with water.

Wonderingly the Ranger stared at the singular contraption. What was the idea? Was it to torture him with the sight of water out of reach while he suffered the pangs of thirst? If that was it, why such an elaborate arrangement? One filled bottle would serve the purpose just as well. Already he was conscious of acute thirst and he knew as the day wore on and he broiled helpless on the scorching sands, his pains would increase. But still the thing didn't make sense.

With a curse of exasperation, he tugged at the thongs that held his wrists. The chords cut into his flesh, and that was all. He could move his fingers, his whole hand, in fact, but his arms were securely held. His head he could not move at all. His body but little. Feet and legs were likewise held rigid.

With a rush of memory, he recalled the dark, savage face of the man who had lured him into the trap.

"It was that little hellion who tried to knife me that night by the saloon window — Monty's sidekick," he muttered.

Hatfield knew that his case was desperate. Still he did not consider it hopeless. Goldy was free and alive. That he gathered from the conversation of his captors before their departure. The sorrel would come at his whistle and would remain in the vicinity. And he would be conspicuous to anyone riding along the trail. And that trail, while not by any means crowded with wayfarers, *was* used.

A strong man does not die from thirst or exhaustion in a day, or even in several days, although his sufferings may be great. Before the life was baked out of his iron frame, somebody was almost certain to ride the trail. He strove to ease the position of his aching head, and again he stared at the triple pairs of water bottles glittering in the sun, which had passed the zenith and was slanting down the western sky.

There was something disquieting in the glitter of those close-hung pairs. Hatfield vaguely felt that a menace was there — a menace he could not define but was nevertheless very real. That peculiar arrangement was not by chance. A set purpose was evinced in that careful pairing at graduated heights and distances. In his ears suddenly rang a peculiar phrase employed by the deep-voiced speaker —

"The Devil's brandin' irons!" What in hell could *that* mean?

The sun was dropping down the sky. Hatfield gazed at its lower rim through the glass of the topmost bottles. And as he gazed and the sun sank slowly lower, he was conscious of an uncomfortable burning sensation just below his left knee and above the top of his half-boot. He tried to writhe away from it, but could not move his leg. And then, with a gasp of horror, he understood.

The Devil's brandin' irons! The full significance of the fiendish device struck home and his body writhed with horror.

Those bottles filled with water, with the blazing desert sun pouring its rays through them, were nothing but powerful burning glasses, concentrating and directing the sun's rays upon his helpless body!

And with a new thrill of horror, he realized the purpose of that careful spacing in pairs. The scorching pinpoints of fire, travelling slowly up his body were directed toward his eyes. The bottles were so hung that the sinking sun would shine through each pair consecutively and by the time the third set of rays had passed across his face, the sight would be burned from his head.

Madly he strove to wrench his head aside, but it was impossible. Bathed in a cold sweat, he desisted and lay panting, scarcely conscious of the searing pain that was now slowly travelling up his thigh, as the cloth of his overalls charred and smoldered. He strained at wrists and ankles, but the thongs held. His wriggling fingers could not reach the knots. He clawed at the pegs but could secure no purchasing grip. Again he relaxed, his flesh crawling with pain as the points of fire bit deep.

Somewhere behind him sounded a plaintive whinny. Goldy had come forth from among the rocks and was wondering what ailed his master.

Hatfield's lips pursed in the whistle that summoned the horse. It was beyond Goldy's powers of understanding to draw the pegs or bite the cords, but his mere presence would be comforting.

A patter of hoofs sounded and a moment later the big horse thrust his muzzle into Hatfield's palm. With trembling fingers he patted the sorrel's nose.

Goldy snorted and lifted his head. And as

he did so, something trailed across the Ranger's hand. It was the bridle, fallen over the horse's head and hanging from the bit rings.

Absently, Hatfield fingered the leather, clutching at it as the burning pain flowed through his body. Goldy raised his head a little higher and tugged gently. Hatfield instinctively tightened his grip and the sorrel obediently lowered his head again.

Suddenly hope rushed through the Ranger's tortured brain. Frantically, his fingers began to work with the dangling leather. Painfully, slowly, he managed to thrust it under the thong which held his wrist. By a writhing constriction that almost dislocated his wrist he got hold of the loop end and drew a goodly length of the strap under the thong.

Writhing and twisting with numbed fingers, he repeated the process, and again. The points of fire had reached his waist now and his whole body was shuddering with the torture. With the strength and tenacity of despair, he managed to wind the bridle about the peg and under the thong once more. Then he thrust his fingers through the loop, drew the strap taut with the peg as a purchase and shouted frantically to the horse —

"Trail, Goldy!"

The great sorrel threw up his head, snorting as the bit dragged his under jaw down. Hatfield felt a mighty wrench at his wrist and a stabbing pain. Again his voice rang out, urgent, insistent. His face was white with strain, his wrist bones felt as if they were being torn apart, the points of fire were stabbing his ribs.

"Trail, Goldy! Trail!"

Squealing with pain and anger, the sorrel reared high. There was a sucking sound as the peg moved in the sand. Hatfield felt the bones of his wrist grind together. The bridle snapped and cracked.

And then the peg flew from the earth. His right arm free, Hatfield ripped the band from his forehead. To free his neck, his other arm, his body was now but the work of a moment. He beat out the fire that smoldered his overalls and shirt, jerked his ankles free and staggered to his feet, only to fall prone again, retching and gasping, his muscles numbed, cramped, turned to water. It was minutes before he could rise once more, stagger to his horse and ride away from the fiendish contraption that winked and glittered evilly after its escaping victim.

Chapter XIX

Aside from a strained wrist, a gradually receding lump on the back of his head and some burns that answered readily to treatment, Hatfield found himself little the worse for his narrow escape from terrible death. His eyes were bleakly cold, however, as he rode the Lazy H range. He had a new conception of the lengths to which the sinister forces working in the Espantosa country would go to remove an obstacle from their path.

Just another example of the terror weapons they employed. Death sharp and sudden is too common in the rangeland for people to be much affected by it; but death by slow torture and horrible mutilation is something that gives pause to the boldest. Men who were willing to face death without a tremor would nevertheless shrink from coming to grips with an outfit that resorted to such methods. Which was doubtless what the outfit had in mind.

The Lazy H was getting a trail herd together and practically denuding the ranch of salable beefs. Doris Carver had learned that the bank at the county seat held Cal Hudgins' note, secured by the ranch itself, and the note would soon be due.

"It has to be met," she told Hatfield, "or at least the interest and a substantial payment. There is very little money in the bank and the only way to get enough ready cash together is to sell all the stock we can. And the markets are none too good at present."

Hatfield rode to town and had a talk with Jaggers Dunn. Dunn readily agreed to buy the trail herd at current market prices.

"We can use 'em," he said. "Seems these rock busters live on beef and whiskey. Nothing else appeals to them."

Day by day, Hatfield and his "rannies" combed the brakes for strays. The herd grew to sizeable proportions. Finally it was ready and was despatched to Espantosa under the care of several punchers and a trail boss, young Cary Walsh, who had been Tom Gibson's assistant. Gibson, incidentally, still hung between life and death in the railroad hospital. Weak and grim, he refused to discuss his trouble with Al Monty.

"I'll take care of that myself, when I get out of here," he whispered weakly to Hatfield. Hatfield refrained from further questioning until Gibson had gained strength.

"You won't have to worry about your note after you get your check from the railroad," Hatfield assured Doris. "And there's plenty of dogies coming on to take care of a spring herd."

But Doris didn't get her check. Long after midnight, Cary Walsh rode into the ranch house yard, swaying in his saddle, his face crusted with dried blood. Across his saddle bow was draped the unconscious form of one of his punchers.

"The other two boys are out there in the desert," he mumbled to Hatfield before he also lost consciousness. "Hellions come onto us just the other side them chimney rocks — The Devil's Kitchen. Downed Hank and Bill. Plugged Bert here through the body and creased me. When I come to, the herd was gone."

Grim of face, Hatfield, at the head of his remaining cowboys, trailed the stolen herd across the desert and rangeland to the wilderness of thorn and bayonet and naked rock that bordered the Rio Grande. There they lost the trail for many hours, and when they finally recovered it, it led straight to the shallow river and vanished amid the purple mountains of Mexico, where it was hopeless to follow it farther.

"Go see the bank," he told Doris. "Get an extension on that note. There's no reason why they shouldn't give it to you. The spread is still here, and it's valuable. All you need is time."

But Doris rode back from the county seat in a despondent mood.

"The bank no longer holds the note," she told Hatfield. "They sold it, just a few days ago, to a Mr. Cosgrove who is connected with one of the railroads."

"You'll have to see Cosgrove," Hatfield told the girl, but he entertained very little hope that the railroad president would grant an extension.

"*Why* do those hellions want this spread?" he asked himself repeatedly. He was certain the reason meant nothing of good for either the Espantosa country or the C & P railroad. After a lot of hard thinking, he had an idea.

"Unless I'm making a big mistake in judging a man, the old hellion will do it," he decided. "And if he does, it will just about put him in the clear so far as the hell-raising hereabouts is concerned."

Acting on his decision, he rode to see Brush Vane.

Vane greeted the Ranger cordially. After some desultory conversation, Hatfield broached the matter which had brought him to the Slash K. Brush Vane tugged at his moustache and regarded the Ranger thoughtfully.

"The few thousands it will take to secure the spread and give the little lady a chance won't mean anything to you one way or the other, I'm sure," Hatfield persuaded.

Vane grunted explosively, got to his feet and turned to the massive safe which stood in one corner of the room.

"I'll do it," he rumbled. "The gal deserves a chance." He turned, and fixed Hatfield with a truculent eye.

"Only," he growled with emphasis, "I don't want to talk about it — don't want it to get around."

He looked actually embarrassed at the thought that the good he did might be generally known. And at that moment, Hatfield had a new insight into the complex character of Brush Vane. He wondered how many more deeds of generosity and kindness, unknown to people in general, could be credited to the stubborn and arrogant old fighter who was ready at all times to go to any lengths to back up his opinions, right or wrong.

From the big safe, Vane counted out the sum necessary and handed it to the Ranger. At that moment, young Sheldon entered the room and Hatfield had an inspiration. Taking a sheet of paper, he scribbled a word of explanation, folded the note and placed it with the money. He handed both to Sheldon Vane.

"I got a notion it wouldn't be a bad idea for you to take this to the little lady, son," he said.

Sheldon Vane, after the situation had been explained to him, departed with alacrity to saddle his horse. Old Brush grasped his big chin with a meditative forefinger, but offered no comment.

Young Sheldon was still "explaining the situation" to Doris Carver when Hatfield arrived at the Lazy H, long after dark. The Ranger, a sunny light in his green eyes, sought his upstairs sleeping room by way of the kitchen and back stairs.

It was in a much more cheerful mood that Hatfield rode to town a couple of days later. He chuckled at the thought of Cosgrove's rage and discomfiture when Cal Hudgins' note fell due and, instead of the expected foreclosure of the ranch, he would find the face and interest ready for him.

His complacency was short-lived, however. The town was seething. Knots of ranchers and cowboys stood on the corners discussing the latest happening. The air was tense, and ominous with an unvoiced threat.

"It's the big bridge west of town," a bartender explained to the Ranger. "It was dynamited last night. Nothin' left but a mess of twisted beams down to the bottom of the wash. Reckon it just about finishes the C & P's chances of gettin' ahead of the L & W."

"I thought that bridge was guarded, day and night," Hatfield commented.

"It was," the barkeep replied. "They found one of the guards, the feller in the shack at this end. Had a bullet hole between his eyes and a gun in his hand. Found a left foot of another guard. Didn't find nothin' at all of the third feller. His shack was closest to where the charges was set."

"Anything to show who did it?"

The bartender glanced furtively about, decided that nobody was within easy hearing distance, and leaned closer.

"There's talk of lynchin' Brush Vane," he whispered hoarsely. "Believe me there's going to be trouble between the Slash K bunch and the other outfits in the section. That dead guard managed to shoot his gun once before they done for him. He plugged one of the hellions, one of those greasy Yaquis that work in Vane's lumber camp."

"Him bein' a Yaqui don't prove he actually worked for Vane," Hatfield pointed out.

The bartender snorted. "Maybe not, but it's almighty funny, if he didn't, that he'd

have a Cibola Timber Co. payroll number
tag in his pocket!"

Chapter XX

Hatfield learned from the bartender that
the guard's body, and the Yaqui's were at
the coroner's office. He finished his drink
and headed for the office.

The old doctor glanced at him keenly
when he made his request, but readily
granted him permission to examine the bodies.

"When you give that half-breed the once-
over, let's see if you can find out what I
did," he remarked cryptically.

A few minutes later, Hatfield straightened
up beside the Yaqui half-breed's body and
stared at the coroner.

"Doc," he said, "this man was shot after
he was dead."

The coroner nodded. "My sentiments,"
replied. "No bleeding. Edges of the bullet
hole blue, and puckered in a mite. Look at
his head."

Hatfield did so, his deft fingers probing
under the lank greasy hair.

"Skull fractured by a heavy blow," he
decided. "I'd say bone splinters were driven
into the brain. Chances are he died almost

instantly."

"And then had a slug fired through his dead body," said the doctor. "Son, there's something funny about this."

"Damn funny," Hatfield agreed. He stood deep in thought for a moment, then let his gaze rest on the coroner's face.

"Doc," he said, "keep this under your hat for a while, will you?"

The old doctor nodded shortly. "Okay," he agreed, "and when you see Bill McDowell next, ask him if he remembers the time I picked bird shot out of his worthless carcass after old Branch Wesley caught him sparkin' his daughter under a pine tree one moonlit night. Lucky for Bill that Wesley had been out for quail instead of deer! That many buckshot in his hide might have proved inconvenient for even Bill McDowell, though he was about forty years younger in those days."

Hatfield shook with laughter. "I'll tell him," he promised, "and much obliged for keeping quiet all this time. How'd you come to spot me?"

"I was over El Paso way during the Salt War," replied the doctor. "Saw you in action there. You ain't easy to forget. Well, good luck — you'll need it — and I'll keep a tight latigo on my jaw."

Hatfield left the office chuckling, but his face was bleak when he hunted up Jaggers Dunn.

"It's a setback, but we're not licked yet," declared the old fighter. "Lucky it wasn't the long bridge east of town. I've tripled the guards on that."

"Folks appear to be getting pessimistic," observed Hatfield.

"Uh-huh," Dunn agreed. "Somebody's been busy talking up the damage done. You'd think that bridge was a thousand feet long instead of a single span, the things that are being said. And sentiment is sure rising against Brush Vane."

Hatfield nodded, and rode back to the Lazy H ranch house in a very serious mood.

"I've got to do something in a hurry, or all hell's going to bust loose," he told himself. "Well, I've got one more card to play, and if that doesn't prove to be the joker, I'm damned if I know which way to turn."

By a simple process of elimination, Hatfield decided that if the key to the mystery was really hidden on the Lazy H spread, it lay somewhere in grim Espantosa Canyon. But what it could be, he had not the slightest idea. To think there was something of value somewhere in that godforsaken jumble of brush and rocks seemed fantastic; but it was the only section of the range he had not carefully combed.

He had a not unnatural aversion to entering the forbidden gorge. It was there the two railroad police met their terrible end. But on that fact he based his theory, if such a nebulous idea could be called a theory. The logical assumption was that the first guard, a plainsman, had stumbled onto something of interest, and had entered the canyon to verify his findings. And had been intercepted and murdered, as was his brother who trailed him to the gorge.

Which led Hatfield to suspect the canyon might well be guarded.

"And if I get spotted going in there, I'll have a chance of making first-hand acquaintance with Yaqui knife work," he told himself.

With this ominous contingency in mind, he approached the canyon in the dark hours just before dawn, when men sleep the soundest, or, if awake, are likely to be the least alert.

Half a mile from the canyon mouth he dismounted, hobbled Goldy, proceeded to cover the rest of the distance on foot, and with the greatest caution. Finally he was within a hundred yards of the darker mass of shadow that was the canyon mouth. Behind a convenient bush he came to a halt, listening and peering.

The silence remained unbroken. Nor could he see any sign of movement or life. Then abruptly his gaze focused on a spot a little to the right of the north canyon wall and but a few yards from its mouth. In the deeper shadow cast by the rock was a faint glow. So faint, indeed, that it might have been nothing more than the phosphorescence rising from a heap of fungus, or even from a decaying animal; but at that instant a vagrant puff of wind wafted to his nostrils an unmistakable whiff of wood smoke. A fire had evidently burnt to ashes and a few glowing coals.

Hatfield continued his cautious advance, crawling on hands and knees, careful not to make the slightest sound. At length he reached a point not more than a dozen yards from the tiny glow, and again came to a halt, undecided as to what to do. That he was near the almost dead campfire of a watcher or watchers, he was fairly certain. But he had no way of knowing just where the watchers might be posted. And for all he knew they might be wide awake and alert.

As he hesitated, something happened. A

branch of resinous wood of which the stem had been eaten through by the flames, fell upon the ashes of the fire and burnt up with a brilliant light. Hatfield saw a man lying beside the fire, sprawled on blankets he had perhaps thrown off in his sleep. In the brief flicker, he also saw that the man had a dark, hawk-nosed face and lank black hair cut in a square bang. He gripped the butt of a gun with one hand. Doubtless he had been sitting up by the fire when weariness overcame him and he had toppled over on the blankets. There was no one else in sight.

The flame flickered out; only the faint glow remained.

Hatfield lay motionless, pondering how to make the most of the opportunity that had suddenly presented itself. If he could capture the watcher and scare him into talking, he might gain valuable information, perhaps the solution of the mystery. But how to capture him? If he tried to creep up on the Yaqui, he might wake up. Very probably he would, for such people, like dogs, mostly sleep with one eye open. And he'd have a good chance of getting the gun into action before Hatfield could dash it from his hand.

Clouds banked in the west suddenly broke and let through a shimmer of wan light from a low-lying, gibbous moon. By the pale glimmer, Hatfield saw that just beyond where the man lay, thick brush grew to within a few yards of the campfire. Before the moon drifted behind another cloud, he was stealing softly back the way he came. He made a wide circle and gained the growth back of the camp. In the east the sky was brightening. The stars flickering between the drifting clouds were dwindling. Soon it would be light. Hatfield again took to his hands and knees and crept slowly and with infinite care through the belt of brush. Finally he reached the last straggling fringe of growth. Only a few yards distant was the shadowy form of the sleeping Yaqui.

Hatfield waited a few minutes for the light to strengthen a bit. Then he stood up and began stealing forward, hand hovering close to his gun. And the unexpected happened. His full weight came down on a crooked stick hidden by fallen leaves. It broke with a crack like a pistol shot.

The Yaqui came to his feet like a released spring. Hatfield saw the gleam of steel and jerked his Colt. The two guns blazed together.

Hatfield felt the wind of the passing slug. The Yaqui crumpled up like a sack of old clothes, sprawled on his blankets and lay still, Hatfield's two bullets laced through his heart. Hatfield leaped back into the growth and for long minutes stood motionless, peering and listening. He was taking no chances against the man possibly having a companion somewhere nearby.

But as the light strengthened, nothing happened. Finally he stole forward again. He examined the body and discovered nothing of interest save a surprisingly large sum in gold and silver coin, in the dead man's pockets.

"Bastard's been doing all right by himself," he muttered as he cast about for a place to conceal the body. "Another half-breed. Wonder who he works for?"

He found a deep crack at the base of the cliff face. Into this he stuffed the body, tumbling the blankets, then stones, on top of it. Then he set out to locate the dead man's horse. He found it without much difficulty, tethered in a nearby thicket. A shaggy, half-wild-looking little beast, it was docile enough. He removed the rig, concealing it under a pile of brush, and turned the animal loose to graze, confident it would fend for itself. Then, with dawn streaking the sky in rose and gold, he hurried back to where he left Goldy. He mounted the sorrel and rode into the canyon.

Closer inspection showed the gorge even

more unprepossessing than when viewed from a distance. The level floor, which had a slight inward slope, was littered with smooth and rounded boulders between which grew patches of thorny growth. The walls were basaltic and devoid of mineral content. It would have been hard to imagine a bleaker or more unprofitable terrain.

"Been a lot of water run through here at one time, from the look of those rocks," Hatfield decided as Goldy slipped and floundered on the inhospitable pebbles.

But at present the only water in evidence was a little stream fed by the overflow of a spring which gushed from under the north wall and wound toward the inner depths of the canyon.

As he progressed, slowly, studying his surroundings with minute care, Hatfield recalled hearing that in the old days, marauding Apache bands used to hole up in the canyon.

"Should have been easy to smoke them out, though," he mused. "They say this thing is a box, and if the end wall is as steep as the side ones, there'd be no climbing it."

The end wall of the box, which he reached a couple of hours later, after a ride totally devoid of results, proved to be just that — a towering stretch of cliff only broken by a cleft a dozen or so feet in width and perhaps twice that in height, into which the stream disappeared.

Hooking a long leg over the saddle horn, Hatfield disgustedly rolled a cigarette with the fingers of his left hand, snapped a match and lighted it. Nothing could have been more meticulous than his inspection of the canyon, and he had discovered exactly — nothing.

As he smoked, his gaze roved over the desolate prospect. Suddenly his eyes narrowed with interest. Over to one side, near the left bank of the stream, appeared several blackened stones arranged in a regular pattern. He spoke to Goldy and rode forward to investigate. His initial surmise was quickly proven correct. The stones were fire-blackened. He was gazing at the site of a camp. Littered about was the debris that indicated the spot had been used more than once and by several persons.

"Now what the devil?" Hatfield wondered. "Been horses here, too."

He dismounted and probed about, unearthing several rusty tin cans, now empty, a couple of whiskey bottles and some charred beef bones. He raised his eyes and gazed at the end wall of the canyon, vainly seeking an answer to the puzzles that piled one upon another.

Beyond the beetling cliff rose the towering battlements of the Espantosa Hills, the grim barrier that pack trains and wagon trains had cursed in the old days, and which now the rival railroads cursed with equal fervor. For the iron hills formed the insurmountable barrier around which the railroads were forced to detour in a giant curve that accounted for more than a hundred miles of slow and costly construction. With an oath, Hatfield returned to his more immediate surroundings. Why, he wondered, had somebody made camp in this desolate spot? A camp that, it appeared, had been maintained for several days. From the appearance of some of the tins, he judged they had lain there for six or eight months, maybe more. Still others were quite new.

Not knowing what else to do, he continued to poke about the camp site. And then he discovered something that quickened his interest to a white heat. Lying half-buried in a mound of ashes was a slim steel rod about fifteen inches long, pointed at one end and with a ring formed by a bend of the metal at the other.

Hatfield instantly recognized the thing for what it was — the spike used by chain men to hold one end of an engineer's chain, or a surveyor's tape, in position while the chain was stretched to another spike some distance away. By successive stretchings of the graduated chain or tape, distances between points could be accurately measured.

"Some jigger used it to poke the fire and dropped it and forgot it," he explained to Goldy, who nodded his head gravely in apparent understanding.

"Horse," Hatfield continued, "I still don't know what the answer is, but I'm beginning to get a notion. It's beginning to look like somebody ran a surveyor's line up this crack in the hills. If that's so, there should be markings somewhere. Let's see what we can find out."

With an engineer's knowledge, he quickly decided on the probable location of the line, if there was one. He went over the ground with painstaking care. Suddenly he uttered an exultant exclamation.

On the flat surface of a stone, tiny figures had been chiseled.

After that, it was easy. Measuring distances with an experienced eye, he traced the line back toward the mouth of the canyon. As he drew nearer the mouth, the figures became smaller, and were usually concealed to remain inconspicuous. Hatfield turned and hurried back to where Goldy contentedly cropped grass. This time he worked toward the box end of the canyon. Near the cleft into which the stream ran he discovered the last markings. He straightened his aching back and stared at the opening in the cliff face.

"I'm beginning to get it — I hope," he told the sorrel. "Well, there's just one way to make sure. You take it easy for a while, feller. If I don't come back, you'll know I made a mistake of some kind."

He prowled about in a thicket of evergreens that grew nearby and cut a number of dry and resinous branches. When a match was set to the end of one, it burned satisfactorily, affording considerable light. Holding it high, and with replenishments under his arm, Hatfield stepped into the shallow waters of the stream and entered the cleft.

For a dozen paces or so, the cleft retained a uniform height and width. Then it abruptly widened to a good thirty feet. The roof rose until Hatfield could barely see the overhanging stone in the flicker of his torch.

Straight ahead stretched the dark corridor, its floor of smooth rock, as were the side walls. Hatfield quickly decided that the bore had been formed by a great volume of water eating its way through a softer strata hundreds of thousands, perhaps even millions of years before.

The cave changed direction slightly now and then, but its general trend continued due west.

It was an eerie sensation, groping through the bowels of the earth with only the whisper of the little stream and the sputter of the torch for company. Although he knew perfectly well to the contrary, Hatfield could not conquer the feeling that he was covering endless miles through the frightful dark, all the more so because his progress was necessarily slow. Not only had he to keep a sharp watch for possible pitfalls in the rock floor, but he had also constantly to scan the wall by his elbow, searching for the survey figures chiseled in the stone. He found them regularly spaced and thus was able to estimate accurately the distance he covered.

But nevertheless the disquieting feeling persisted. Perhaps the figures were wrong. Perhaps his own estimate of distance covered was in error. He knew darn well it wasn't, but as the intangible darkness beat against the tiny circle of dim radiance cast by his torch, he was forced to combat a tendency to sheer panic that threatened to overwhelm him. He suffered an almost uncontrollable impulse to run madly along the black tunnel, seeking frantically for the light that seemed to have been left behind forever. Muttering an oath, he deliberately slowed his pace more than was necessary and trudged on grimly, peering at the stone barrier that walled him in, grunting with satisfaction when his eyes lit on the figures chiseled on its surface.

Another disquieting thought intruded to make matters worse. Perhaps he had turned into some side passage and was now wandering through a labyrinth of galleries in which he could easily become totally lost. The torches had burned faster than he anticipated and he had but two left. Let the terrible darkness close in and even his uncanny plainsman's sense of direction could become confused. He breathed deeply of the heavy air, muggy, slightly mephitic, such as could be expected in lost, lightless grottos far from the bright sun and the happy winds. His footsteps threw back sodden, dreary echoes from the encroaching stone. A grim, chilling phrase began beating in his brain —

Cramped in a coffin, and the clods falling, falling!

"A little more of this and I *will* go loco," he growled, and quickened his pace.

According to the survey figures chiseled on the stone, he had covered something less than seven-eighths of a mile when the cave began curving gently. For a couple of hundred yards the shallow arc continued, then again the bore swung back to almost due west. And Hatfield saw light ahead.

It was gray, shadowy light, but a welcome relief from the total blackness. Almost at a run he pressed forward. The wan glow increased in strength, but still held to the sober gray that gave an impression of heaviness as if only the turgid dregs of light could penetrate to these dreary depths.

Which was exactly the case. A few moments later Hatfield emerged from the cave or tunnel and found himself at the bottom of a frightful gorge, the sheer sides of which rose a full thousand feet to where a narrow ribbon of blue sky seemed to press down on the crests of the overhanging cliffs.

The canyon trended nearly due west until the rocky walls drew together in the distance. It was almost solidly floored with rock, only a scattering of dead-looking growth breaking the flat monotony.

It was a most forbidding prospect, but as he gazed upon it, Hatfield's eyes glowed triumphantly.

"Looks like I've got the answer to everything," he muttered, "but I've got to make sure."

Without hesitation he turned and plunged back into the cave. He did not even bother to light a torch, knowing that the way was clear. It was quite different, hurrying back the way he had come, from groping his way along with only vague conjectures to support him. Only a few minutes elapsed before he was swinging into the saddle and urging Goldy into the cleft.

Goldy didn't like it, and said so with explosive snorts and petulant tossing head; but he obeyed orders and ambled along through the darkness at a good pace. They left the cave and headed down the gorge.

Mile after mile Hatfield rode. For a few moments, when the sun was directly overhead, a thin, dazzling line of golden lights pierced the gloomy depths; but it was soon gone as the sun passed across the zenith and the somber shadows resumed.

But when they at last reached the far distant western mouth of the canyon, red-golden light was pouring a flood of brilliance into the gorge. Ahead, stretching on to the setting sun, was an illimitable vista of level rangeland.

Hatfield rode on a little way, turned in his saddle and gazed back at the battlements of the Espantosa Hills — hills that now lay to the east. They had passed completely through the sprawling range.

Hatfield's heart beat exultantly. The mystery was no longer a mystery. He had the solution, and the reason for the sinister happenings that had plagued the Espantosa country.

"No wonder Cosgrove, or, rather, the man who dominates Cosgrove, was willing to destroy and murder to attain his ends," he told the horse. "Here it is — a direct, water-level route through the hills. Easily accessible to either road, and will cut off a hundred miles, maybe more, of slow and costly construction. L & W stock would have shot up sky-high, and the holder of a large block of that stock would have realized a fortune in profits. Well, there'll be some changes now."

Hatfield had coffee, bacon, and some flour in his saddle pouches, along with a small skillet and a little flat bucket. He rode back up the canyon till he found a suitable spot and made camp for the night. He lit a fire and quickly threw together a simple but adequate meal — bacon, a dough cake fried in the fat, and hot coffee. Then, after smoking a cigarette or two in the deepening gloom, he stretched out beside the fire with his saddle for a pillow and slept until the dawn turned the ribbon of sky to flame.

Then he saddled up and headed for the Lazy H at a fast pace. He approached the east mouth of Espantosa Canyon wearily; but all was peaceful there. The ashes of the Yaqui watchman's fire lay dead and deserted. Hatfield rode on across the sun-golden rangeland.

He reached the ranch house shortly after noon, cheerful and confident, ready for his final move in the grim chess game in which lives were the pawns and death the penalty for misplay.

As he rode into the ranch-house yard, he met Doris Carver, riding swiftly from the corral. The girl's face was white and strained.

"A Mexican wrangler just brought the news from town," she gasped in reply to Hatfield's question. "All the ranch owners of the district are gathering there. They think the C & P directors may vote to abandon the new line and that the investors here will lose all they put in the project. They blame Brush Vane and his outfit for the trouble. They're going to lynch him and his son and drive his outfit from the country. Vane and his men are in Espantosa and say they'll fight to a finish. There are bound to be killings. Oh, can't you do something? I am going to town to see if I can help — the

— the —"

"That's right, Ma'am," Hatfield interrupted gently. "Stick by your man, right or wrong, only this time he's right!"

He wheeled the sorrel toward the Espantosa Trail.

"I'll ride with you!" shrilled the girl, divining his purpose.

"You can ride *after* me!" Hatfield flung over his shoulder. "Trail, Goldy!"

CHAPTER XXI

In the open space before the Espantosa lockup, a tight group of men were gathered. Brush Vane was there, his heavy face expressing more concern than was its wont. On one side stood his son, Sheldon Vane, pale but determined. On the other was Sheriff Nat Rider, his moustache bristling, his eyes bitterly cold. One gnarled hand rested on his gun butt. Spread out on either side were a dozen of the Slash K cowboys, faces bleak, eyes glinting in the shadow of their hats. Hands by their sides, tense, alert, they faced the hard-faced crowd of half a hundred ranchers and riders who thronged the other side of the street. In the rear of this group was Jaggers Dunn, red-faced and fuming, a pistol barrel pressed against his ribs.

And a little distance up the street, stood three men, watching proceedings with sardonic interest. One was Bijah Cosgrove. Beside him stood the dark, saturnine Al Monty in his funereal black. The third member of the trio was a wiry little half-breed with nervous hands and a twitching face. All three were unnoticed by the tense groups that faced each other across the dusty street. Sheriff Rider was speaking, his voice rasping harshly, his big chin thrust forward.

"I won't do it," said the sheriff. "If a proper warrant is swore out, I'll serve it on this man and I'll lock him up same as I would anybody else; but I ain't turnin' nobody over to the mob. You fellers has gone loco. This'll end in a dozen killin's if you don't use some sense."

An angry roar went up from the other side of the street.

"We're givin' you one minute to surrender, Vane," barked a big cowman. "When that minute is up, we're comin' to get you!"

On both sides of the street was a simultaneous clutching at weapons. Sheriff Rider tensed. Brush Vane wet his lips with a nervous tongue. The Slash K punchers

223

spread out a little.

Down the street sounded a sudden thunder of fast hoofs. Monty, Cosgrove and the half-breed, from their point of vantage farther up the street, recognized the rider first.

"It's him!" whimpered the scrawny half-breed. He broke into excited Spanish. *Madre de Dios!* — that one bears the life that is charmed. None may kill him!"

"Shut up!" the dark Monty rasped hoarsely. "Start movin' when I do; shoot fast, and then cut and ride for the Border. That hellion's bringing trouble. Get over to one side, Bije."

Up the street crashed a great sorrel horse. With Goldy in full stride. Hatfield swung to the ground and strode fearlessly between the two groups. His face was bleak, his eyes coldly gray. On his broad breast gleamed a silver star set on a silver circle, the feared and honored badge of the Texas Rangers. His voice rolled in thunder through the sudden silence.

"In the name of the State of Texas! This is an unlawful gathering. Disperse and go about your business in an orderly manner."

For a moment the stunned silence continued. Then a gabble of voices arose.

"Good gosh!" somebody bawled. "That

feller's a Ranger!"

Old Sam Gerard let out a wild whoop.

"Didn't I tell you so, Mack?" he bellowed. "Didn't I tell you he was a Ranger? And, goddamn it! — the Lone Wolf! Ever hear tell of him, boys?"

They had. Not a man there but who had heard of the Ranger whose exploits of daring were legend in the Southwest. And they knew well the price that would be paid for resistance to Ranger authority. There would be bullets, swift and sure, to the hearts and brains of some, and vengeance equally swift and sure for all, when Roaring Bill McDowell and his "Gentlemen in the White Hats" rode into the Espantosa country with flaming rifles to exact the terrible payment for a Ranger slain.

The front line of the mob shredded out. Men shuffled back, some grinning sheepishly, on their faces an expression of relief. Now that the fires of anger had cooled somewhat, men realized that things had gotten out of hand, that what they had contemplated doing was not justified by common sense. With Ranger authority in their midst, there would be impartial investigation, and justice.

After that single, sweeping glance of contempt, Hatfield ignored the mob. His attention was centered on the three men a little way up the street. He strode forward, his hands at his sides, his eyes never leaving the unsavory trio. His voice rang out again, edged with steel —

"In the name of the State of Texas, I arrest for the destruction of the railroad bridge, and for murder, Bijah Cosgrove and — Austin Flint! Anything you say —"

The final words were drowned by Cosgrove's high-pitched gabbling scream of terror. The railroad president seemed to shrink and shrivel. He whirled around and started to run.

Al Monty stood rigid, his dark face working, his eyes terrible. He rasped a curse and his hands moved like the sidewinder's deadly, lashing stroke. His guns flamed and roared as they cleared leather. Beside him, the little half-breed was shooting with both hands.

Men saw Hatfield's hat move on his head. Saw a red streak leap across one bronzed cheek, his left sleeve twitch as if plucked by ghostly fingers.

Then one of the "breed's" glittering eyes went blank. At the same instant Monty pitched forward on his face.

Quick-thinking Sheldon Vane bounded after the fleeing Cosgrove, caught him and hurled him to the ground.

Hatfield holstered his guns and walked slowly forward. His face was suddenly tired and lined. He gazed down at the two bodies. The "breed" was dead, blood and brains still oozing from the gaping hole that the emerging slug had torn in the back of his head. Monty lay face downward, his life draining out through his shattered lungs.

Brush Vane was plucking at Hatfield's sleeve. "My God, son!" he exclaimed. "Do you mean to tell me that hellion is Austin Flint? Why, look at his hair, and the color of his skin!"

Hatfield knelt beside the dying man and gently turned him over on his back. The glazing eyes glared up into his, then became fixed and immovable. Monty was dead.

Hatfield unbuttoned the dead man's shirt. Vane swore in astonishment. The skin below the line of dark stain showed surprisingly white.

"And look at the roots of his hair," Hatfield added, flipping off Monty's hat.

"By gosh! It's yellow!" exploded Vane.

"Exactly," Hatfield nodded. "An old trick. I've used the stuff a few times myself. A simple Apache brew from herbs and berries. They used it in the course of their ceremonial dances, to protect the skin from their war paint, which always had a cinnebar base and was apt to cause sores. Plain water won't touch it, but strong soap removes it in a few minutes."

"But why in blazes would Flint do such a thing?" asked Jaggers Dunn, who, with the sheriff had joined them. Rider's deputy and Sheldon Vane had meanwhile hurried Cosgrove off to the lockup.

"Two reasons, I believe," Hatfield replied. "First, as Vane's timber cruiser it allowed him to get the lowdown on things and to keep in touch with his Yaqui and Apache "breeds" he'd planted with the Cibola Timber Company. Those "breeds" were part of a gang he'd headed farther west, that went in for wide-looping, smuggling and stage robberies. Second, as I told you, Mr. Dunn, Flint was a gunfighter. He had the killer yen. As Monty he was able to play the part he liked, which he couldn't do as Austin Flint, respectable business man."

"But how did Cosgrove get mixed up with him, anyhow?"

"I think I know," Hatfield replied, "but we'll make sure. I want to have a little talk with Cosgrove. Let's all drop over to the sheriff's office."

After talking with Cosgrove, in his cell, Hatfield returned to the office.

"I guessed right," he said. "Cosgrove and Flint knew each other back East. Flint was another political thug and triggerman. They were in jail together. Later, after Cosgrove got into the railroad business and Flint drifted west, they kept in touch with each other. When Cosgrove got the idea of bucking the C & P for the southwest haulage, he contacted Flint and set him to work over here. Flint was the stronger character and soon had Cosgrove under his thumb. When he first landed here, he saw there'd be money in timber and proceeded to get hold of all he could. Cosgrove is no lily-white, but Flint urged him into things he'd never thought of doing himself. And here's the solution to the whole mystery:

In a few terse sentences he acquainted his hearers with what he had discovered in Espantosa Canyon.

"Well, I'll be damned!" exclaimed Brush Vane. "I knew about that crack in the hills all along. Rode through there once, years ago. Heard about it from an old Apache who worked for me."

"And because of that knowledge, you came darn near getting yourself killed," Hatfield remarked grimly. "They were scared you might remember, and spill the beans. Flint learned about it from an Apache, too.

In the old days the raiding Apaches did head for Espantosa Canyon. But they didn't hole up there, as people thought. They kept right on going by way of the cave and canyon through the hills, coming out on the grassland to the west. Flint, of course, realized the value of that passage to the railroads. He tried to get control of it. But Cal Hudgins, whose holdings took in Espantosa Canyon, wouldn't sell. Flint was balked. So he got rid of Hudgins and shot his range boss, Tom Gibson, after Hudgins' niece showed up and wouldn't sell, either."

"But why didn't they invoke Eminent Domain and get control that way?" asked Jaggers.

Hatfield smiled. "You can't invoke Eminent Domain without attendant publicity. That's what they didn't want. Hudgins wouldn't sell to Cosgrove, but he would have sold to you without argument."

"Guess you're right," admitted Dunn. "How'd you catch on Monty was Flint?"

Hatfield rolled a cigarette before replying.

"I got suspicious of Flint when I heard him talk," Hatfield replied. "He claimed to have been born and brought up in the Texas Panhandle country. But I never knew a born Texan to say 'callate,' 'railrud,' ' 'low' or 'town meeting.' Those are Down East expressions. And I've learned that when a man tries to conceal his origins, he'll bear watching. So I got to puzzling over Flint. He had me guessing for quite awhile. Everything wrong pointed to Brush Vane. When ever one of those *"breeds"* was downed in the course of some skullduggery, for instance, he had a Cibola Lumber Company payroll tag in his pocket. The last one, incidentally, the one picked up by the dynamited bridge, was planted to throw suspicion on Vane. It's an old owlhoot trick, and usually effective, getting decent people on the prod against one another. Distracts attention from what is really going on. When I shook hands with Monty up at the lumber camp, I noticed something. The cuticle of his nails showed a line of pink. As I said, I've used that dye myself, and I always found it darn hard to get it to take on the cuticle. Flint slipped a little there, as the owlhoot brand always does."

"He don't miss anything," chuckled the sheriff.

"You learn to look out for the small things in Ranger work," Hatfield said. "Well, right there I knew Monty wasn't what he set up to be. And I'd heard him use a few expressions similar to those Flint used. And when I learned the man buying up L & W stock

231

called himself Albert Stone, I was sure of my man. That's another peculiarity of owl-hoots. They usually take false names that are similar to their own. Flint had already become the chief suspect by process of elimination. Everybody else had managed to get in the clear, one way or another. Then when I found the tunnel through the hills, everything was clear."

He paused, smiling down at his listeners. "So that's about all," he concluded. "Mr. Dunn, you can go ahead and build a rail-road, and take over the L & W as a feeder, if you've a mind to. Cosgrove won't have anything to say about it for a long, long time. He can trade a job of building railroad for one busting rocks behind a stone wall, if he doesn't stretch rope for murder. And, Mr. Vane, I think you've had a lesson that will stick with you for quite a spell. Give up playing God, suh. That's too big a job for any man to tackle.

"Sorry I can't stay for the wedding, Shel-don, but Captain Bill will have another little chore lined up for me by the time I get back to the post. I'll see you all later. Suppose I'll have to come back for Cosgrove's trial."

They watched him ride away, into the red blaze of the setting sun.

The Lone Wolf was on the trail again.

The employees of Thorndike Press hope you have enjoyed this Large Print book. All our Thorndike, Wheeler, and Kennebec Large Print titles are designed for easy reading, and all our books are made to last. Other Thorndike Press Large Print books are available at your library, through selected bookstores, or directly from us.

For information about titles, please call:
  (800) 223-1244

or visit our Web site at:
  http://gale.cengage.com/thorndike

To share your comments, please write:
  Publisher
  Thorndike Press
  10 Water St., Suite 310
  Waterville, ME 04901